Praise for **Other People's Baggage**

"Lost luggage has never been this fun! With well-drawn characters, *Other People's Baggage* is your first class ticket to three fast-paced adventures full of mystery, murder, and magic."

– Elizabeth Craig,
Author of the Southern Quilting Series

"What do you get when you mix Doris Day with a dash of Texas two-step, then stir in a smidgen of Edinburgh, secret chambers, and magic? A recipe for fun entitled, *Other People's Baggage*. Although mixed up luggage is the thread that connects this trio of globetrotting novellas, it's snappy dialogue, clever storytelling, and charming characters that are the real common denominators...I'm already hooked on their three new mystery series, and I've only read the prequels!"

– Maddy Hunter,
Bestselling Author of the Passport to Peril Mystery Series

"Those who enjoy travel and mysteries like myself will definitely enjoy reading *Other People's Baggage*, three novellas about female sleuths who solve two thefts and a murder while coping with an airport mixing up their three bags. The mix-ups are a creative theme for tying the stories together, and I loved seeing how each sleuth dealt with the problem. A very fun collection!"

– Beth Groundwater,
Author of the Claire Hanover Gift Basket Designer
and RM Outdoor Adventures Mystery Series

Three Interconnected Mystery Novellas

OTHER PEOPLE'S
BAGGAGE

Kendel Lynn, Gigi Pandian
& Diane Vallere

HENERY PRESS

OTHER PEOPLE'S BAGGAGE
A Henery Press Mystery Collection

First Edition
Trade paperback edition | December 2012

Henery Press
www.henerypress.com

Cover Artwork by Fayette Terlouw

ISBN-13: 978-1-938383-10-6

Printed in the United States of America

OTHER PEOPLE'S
BaGGaGe

In the not-so-distant past, a major storm coupled with a computer glitch stranded thousands of passengers at the Dallas/Fort Worth airport. As the passengers searched for their mislabeled luggage and scrambled for new flight connections, three lives intersected thanks to identical vintage suitcases. These are the stories of what happened when three women with a knack for solving mysteries each picked up the wrong bag...

PART 1:
MIDNIGHT ICe

A Mad for Mod Mystery Novella (prequel to *Pillow Stalk*)

by Diane Vallere

PART 2:
SWITCH BaCK

An Elliott Lisbon Mystery Novella (prequel to *Board Stiff*)

by Kendel Lynn

PART 3:
FOOL'S GOLD

A Jaya Jones Treasure Hunt Mystery Novella (prequel to *Artifact*)

by Gigi Pandian

PART 1:
MIDNIGHT ICE

A Mad for Mod Mystery Novella (prequel to *Pillow Stalk*)

by Diane Vallere

ONE

I started my getaway on the floor. And by floor, I mean the beige speckled linoleum tile squares that covered the ground by the Monterey Airport baggage claim. A fragile-looking Chihuahua broke free from the grasp of a young girl and ran over to sniff me. The girl moved toward the dog but her dad held her hand tightly. She started to cry. I tried to roll over again, but a stab of pain shot through my knee cap and I flopped back onto my butt. My face flushed with embarrassment, not over the fact that a group of official looking men and a steady stream of travelers had seen the turquoise cotton panties I wore under my early sixties aqua sheath dress but because I knew I needed to ask someone for help getting back up and I didn't like to ask for help strangers, official-looking or otherwise.

The passengers around me gave me a one foot berth, enough to indicate I was woman down, but not enough to give up their prime spot for retrieving their luggage as it came off the beltline.

A man in a black suit approached me. He corralled my crutches to the side with his foot, then stood behind me and put his hands under my arms. I held the end to the Chihuahua's leash in my hand as I stood, then crutched to the little girl, her dog trailing behind me, and returned her charge. The official-looking man stood by the luggage conveyor belt watching me.

"You okay?" asked the man who had helped me up. Now that we were face to face I noticed he was not much taller than I was. He was tan, with a mole under his left eye. His longish sandy-blond hair was parted on the side and tucked behind his ears. He held a piece of paper that said Day.

"Reservation for Day? That's me. Give me a second to get my suitcase and we can go."

The crowd of travelers had thinned significantly, and only a few bags were left on the luggage belt. My blue and white 1950's hardback suitcase was one of them. I anchored the crutches under my arms and moved closer to the belt. It didn't take a rocket scientist to realize I couldn't pick up my suitcase while balanced on the crutches.

"Which one's yours?"

"The blue and white one," I answered.

He pulled the suitcase from the conveyor belt and turned away from me. He walked fast, faster than I would have expected considering he was well aware of my crutch-handicap, I didn't ask him to slow down. I was going to function the way I always functioned, post-knee injury or no post-knee injury.

The driver and I reached the parking lot within twenty seconds of each other. When I arrived at the car he was shutting the trunk with my luggage inside. He opened the back door of the sedan and waved for me to go inside.

"Ms. Day," he said with a nod.

"Actually, it's not Day, it's Night." His eyebrows and his mouth turned down at the same time, as if little puppet strings from somewhere below us controlled is expression. "Madison Night," I added, turning my introduction into a James Bond-ism.

"Madison Night?" he checked his clipboard. "I have a reservation for D. Day."

"I didn't want to travel under my own name. If you check your paperwork, you'll find my name matches the name on the credit card used to hold the reservation." His suspicion was obvious but I ignored it. My knee throbbed from the fall by the baggage claim and now, to add insult to injury, my underarms ached from the speed-crutching I'd done to keep up with him.

I pulled the crutches out from under me and pushed them into the back seat, then followed them into the dark black interior. I slid my license and credit card from the wallet inside the quilted leather bag I had slung across my body and waited for the inevitable request to see them. Instead, he shut my door and walked around the other side, then climbed in behind the wheel.

"Forgive me, Ms. Night. When I saw a reservation for D. Day, going to Carmel By-The-Sea, well, I thought I might be having a brush with fame."

"To tell you the truth, Doris Day is why I'm going to Carmel. She's like a—" I stopped talking abruptly, realizing I didn't know how to finish the sentence to a stranger.

"You know her?" he asked.

"She's kind of like a Godmother."

"So I guess I am having that brush with fame. Doris Day's Goddaughter."

I knew right then and there I should have corrected him, let him know I didn't really know Doris Day. That if she was like a godmother, it was of the fairy Godmother type. Ever since I'd learned of her in my teenage years, after discovering we shared the birthday of April third, I'd developed more than a passing interest in the actress, copying her look, her style, and most of all, her integrity. It was that bubbly personality that had carried her through so many tragedies in her own life that I responded to, that I used as a guide for how to live my own life. When I'd gotten out of the hospital in Pennsylvania, knowing I was alone in my recovery, I knew there was one place I could go to restore my emotional strength and start to move on.

Cypress Inn, Doris Day's hotel in Carmel By-The-Sea.

I'd booked the reservation while on my way to the Philadelphia airport. My timing, though spontaneous, was perfect. The hotel was under renovation so it would be ready for the annual art festival in a few months. Something about the renovation rang a bell with me, but I didn't know what. I'd read off my credit card number to hold a room, then sat back and tried to forget why I wanted to get away.

We arrived at the hotel twenty minutes later. Traces of the pain killer I'd taken between flights at the Dallas airport were still in my system and the grogginess hadn't yet worn off. I was eager to get to my room and finally relax.

I checked in relatively quickly while a porter stood nearby, waiting for my room number to be assigned so he could deliver my bag. Posters from Doris Day movies lined the walls of the concierge desk and the small reception area. Two chubby ladies in pastel linen suits walked behind me, both led by dogs on leashes. The woman in the lilac wore a matching hat with a bit of netting over her face. Her dog, a Yorkie, pranced next to a white Peek-a-poo who belonged to the woman in sea-foam green. Nearby, a cat was curled up on a floral sofa, napping in a spot of sunshine.

"Ms. Night, your room is 319," said the handsome concierge. A plastic nametag reading Harrison was pinned to the lapel of his light tan suit. He had salt and pepper hair that looked as if it had been recently cut, revealing a small border of untanned skin by his hairline. If he were the sort to dye his hair he would have looked younger, but I immediately liked that he wasn't and didn't. "Lionel will take your luggage to your room for you. We have sherry at four every afternoon in the lounge, jazz in the courtyard from seven to ten, and Terry's Lounge is open until eleven for dinner, or drinks if you fancy a nightcap."

"Thank you," I said to Harrison. Lionel went one direction with my suitcase and I went the other.

The elevator lobby was at the end of a small carpeted hallway that ran past the restaurant. A large mirror hung on the wall above a marble table with a hotel phone and an ugly, squat, adobe-colored lamp that failed to complement the hotel's mid-century modern décor. The lamp hadn't been turned on and the small waiting area was dark.

I felt for the knob on the lamp and clicked it repeatedly but nothing happened.

Voices from men waiting for their elevator floated to me from around the corner. They seemed not to notice my presence.

"She's here. I haven't seen her yet, but she's here. The message said she'd be available tonight, after ten," said the shorter man.

"Is that when you're going to see her?" asked the man in the suit. "And what about the last guy? Is he showing up to make sure she's in good hands?"

"I hope so. I've been waiting a long time. I hope she's as pretty as she sounds."

I crept forward and looked at the men. The taller one was in a grey suit with a white shirt unbuttoned at the neck. He wore glasses without the rims, and smelled like expensive aftershave. The other man, shorter but more muscular, had on a striped shirt and tie under his sport coat and blue jeans.

I tried to pretend I wasn't listening in on their conversation, considering they didn't know I was standing there. I half-turned, thought about stepping back into the shadows until after they'd gotten on the elevator, but that's when they spotted me.

Grey suit nodded his head at me. "I bet that sounded funny to you, ma'am," he said.

"To be honest, I wasn't paying attention. I'm a little lost in my thoughts," I lied.

"First time in Carmel?" asked Blue Jeans.

"Yes."

"You picked a nice hotel. Doris Day's hotel, but by the looks of you, I'm betting you already knew that."

I looked past the men to my reflection in a decorative mirror. He was right. In my vintage aqua double knit sheath dress and coordinating ivory jacket lined in matching aqua silk, I looked like an Avon Lady from the early sixties, not the carefree vacationer I was trying to be. But this was how I was comfortable, in my vintage ensembles. Drop me in a mall and I'd have a panic attack trying to put together the kind of outfit that might be featured in a recent fashion magazine.

I ran my fingers through my short blond hair, trying to bring back the pouf that I'd started with before I'd caught the plane in Dallas. "Your bet would have paid off. I've been a fan of hers my whole life."

"A fan? I would have guessed you're related. You look just like she looks on that poster." He pointed to the *Lover Come Back* poster on the wall. "Minus the silly hat."

The men laughed.

I could have introduced myself. I could have elaborated on Doris Day as style icon. I could have told him I owned that very hat. Instead, when the bell to the elevator chimed, I maneuvered my way inside.

The two men followed.

"What floor?"

"Three," I said. I didn't know whether it was the way I'd left Pennsylvania, like I was running from someone or something, or the fact that grey suit didn't hit another floor's button after he hit the three, that put me on alert.

When the car arrived on the third floor, both men stepped out. Maybe we were all on the third floor, I thought. But when they let me pass them, I knew I was being watched, and I didn't like the feeling. About ten feet down the hall I stopped to study the plastic signs that indicated which room was where, then went the direction opposite 319. The elevator door was still open, but the men weren't in the hallway. I couldn't control the sound of the crutches even though I was on carpet. Plunk, creak, step. Plunk, creak step. As I passed the elevator, I looked inside. The two men stood there, blue jeans on his cell phone. Grey suit smiled at me.

"I got turned around, I guess."

"Happens to me all the time," he replied.

I couldn't be sure, but it seemed like he took his finger off the button and the doors slid shut. I rounded the corner and leaned against the wall, counting silently to myself, waiting to see if the doors would reopen. They didn't.

In a matter of minutes, I arrived at my room. The suitcase sat on a luggage cart by the end of my bed. The sun filtered through the sheer white curtains and I could see the water from my window. I'd requested a room with a view and this room didn't disappoint. I wanted to shower, to change clothes, and to relax on my balcony with a glass of wine from a local vineyard. I wanted to start to forget.

I undid the brass clamps on the suitcase and flipped it open. And that's when I realized I had a whole other set of problems.

TWO

"This is Madison Night in room 319. I just checked in. The wrong suitcase was delivered to my room. Yes, I can hold." I sat on the bed and stared at the neatly folded contents of the suitcase. And by neatly folded, I meant obsessively neat. I knew my spontaneous decision to get out of town had left me packing in a less than orderly fashion, but even if I'd been planning this getaway for a month I would never have packed like this.

While I waited for the concierge to locate Lionel and figure out where my suitcase had gone, I stared at the top layer of the suitcase interior. It was covered in Ziploc baggies, each labeled and numbered. I recognized hair products, cosmetics, and lotions all packed individually. Why would a person separate their toiletries, especially if they checked their luggage? Why use the Ziploc bag at all if you didn't have to go through the security screening with liquids?

"Ms. Night?" said the concierge, returning to the phone.

"Yes?"

"Lionel says that's your bag."

"That is most definitely not my bag," I said.

"Would you like to come down to the lobby and talk to him?"

"I'm on my way."

I left the suitcase open and slipped my feet back into my white sneakers. My underarms were sore from the crutches rubbing the double-knit polyester dress against my skin. I limped a few steps, favoring my injured knee, to test if I could make the trip without the cursed wooden instruments, but it seemed, if I wanted to be mobile, I had no other choice.

Lionel was waiting for me by the concierge desk. The man who had checked me in waved me over. "Ms. Night, I'm sorry for any inconvenience, but Lionel assures me he took your suitcase directly to your room. Isn't that right, Lionel?"

"Yes, ma'am. I noticed the tags on it. I moved here from Dallas, so I was thinking I'd like to ask you what part you're from. You did come from Dallas, didn't you?"

"I connected through Dallas, but I'm not from there. I live in Pennsylvania." Live. Lived. Once lived. I didn't bother explaining my issues with tense or my own question as to whether or not I'd go back.

"Did you check the luggage tag, Ms. Night?"

"No, I'm afraid I didn't. I opened the suitcase and the contents were unfamiliar."

The two men looked at each other. "Would you like us to call the airport for you?" the concierge asked.

"No, I can do that, and I should probably have the tag in front of me when I do so. I'm sorry for the confusion. Good night, gentlemen."

I turned around and went back the direction from which I'd come, back to my room, back to the awesome view and the wrong suitcase. I sat on the bed, then fell backward and spread my arms out to my sides and stared at the ceiling.

I wanted to wash off the day. I limped to the bathroom, where an assortment of shampoo, conditioner, lotion, and soap, but most of all, a post-shower plush white terrycloth robe awaited me. After stripping down to nothing, I stepped in under a hot spray of water, where I stood for the better part of an hour.

I towel-dried and belted myself into the robe, then emerged from the cocoon of steam into my room. The sun was setting, a glow of purple and orange in the sky above the mountainous horizon and deep blue water. I found the mini-bar and poured myself a glass of Sauvignon Blanc, then opened the doors and stood on my balcony. The breeze was cool against my skin. I drank in the air coming off the water, the lingering scent of honeysuckle and grass. This was heaven. This was the most beautiful view I'd seen. No wonder Doris Day had chosen to live here.

I sipped my wine and leaned on the white metal banister. Couples dotted the street, sprinkled with children and dogs. This was a walking town and I was barely able to walk. Not for the first time, I cursed Brad. I cursed the way he'd ended it, two weeks after telling me, one romantic night in the back of Pierot's interior design studio, he wanted us to be together forever. I cursed how I'd skied away from him after he told me he was already married; I cursed the accident that had sent me to the hospital.

A part of me still didn't believe it was over, even if I knew it had to be. That's why I'd left Pennsylvania with a quickly packed suitcase for a spontaneous trip to Carmel, California. I had to go someplace where I knew I wouldn't see him, because the longer I stayed in Pennsylvania, the more I thought I saw him everywhere I went. And the longer I went without running into him, the stronger that feeling became, the feeling I was being watched, that he was there, but not there. I didn't know if it was wishful thinking or paranoia, but I knew I had to get away.

Deep voices pulled me away from the memory of the accident. I looked around, at the balcony to my left and to my right. Both were vacant. The creaking above me let me know my company was one floor up. I sipped the wine and listened to the snippets of conversation.

"The only thing I know is she was supposed to arrive today and we'll see her tonight."

"Do you trust your source?"

"I don't see any choice right now."

"So she's at the hotel. She could be here already. She could be in any one of these rooms and we wouldn't even know it."

"Yeah. We might have walked right past her and not even known. Do you know who brought her?"

There was no answer.

"Doesn't matter. She's going to be in the bar tonight, and that's when we'll grab her."

Grab her. A chill ran down my spine.

"You don't think anybody will notice you grabbing a blonde from the bar?"

"I can't see any other choices." There was a pause. By now I'd identified the voices as the two men from the elevator. "So here's the plan. Get into disguise by nine, meet at the bar at nine-thirty. When she shows up, we hit it and quit it. Until then, it's the friendly stranger routine. got it?"

The friendly stranger routine. That's what I'd allowed myself to believe only moments earlier. I gripped the metal banister harder for balance.

"Hey Louis, did you find out where she's coming from?"

"Someplace on the east coast. I don't know the details, but I know she made a stopover in Dallas."

That's when I dropped the glass.

THREE

"What was that?" asked one of the voices.

I stumbled backward, through the balcony doors. My right hand grabbed at the sheer curtains that blew in and out of the room, steadying myself. I was afraid to be visible. I slid the glass door shut and pulled the cord that blocked the sunlight from the room. I lowered myself to the floor next to the plush Queen Anne chair in the corner.

Minutes later there was a knock on my door. I tried to curl into a ball but my injured knee wouldn't bend. I twisted to my side and lay down against the carpet. The slightest task of breathing in, breathing out, was too loud and threatened to give away my presence.

The knocking started up again. "Ms. Night? This is Jack Jordan, hotel security. I'm here to check on your luggage. Ms. Night, are you in there?"

I wanted to get up, to open the door, to tell this Jack Jordan there were men in the room above me who wanted to grab me at the stroke of ten o'clock, but even as I thought the words, I knew I would sound crazy. There had to be another explanation.

"Ms. Night?" he repeated.

Stop saying my name! I screamed internally. Out loud, I said nothing.

A piece of white paper slipped under my door. I sat on the floor by the arm chair for another two minutes, marked off by the red neon clock that sat on the nightstand next to the bed. Finally, I pushed myself up and retrieved the paper. It was on hotel letterhead.

Dear Ms. Night,

We've been notified of a luggage mix-up at DFW airport thanks to a storm that knocked out their computers. We have no word on where your luggage is or how soon we can get it to you, but we hope to have an answer shortly. In the meantime, please contact our front desk for any toiletries or immediate needs you might discover and we will do our best to accommodate you.

Sincerely,
Jack Jordan
Manager, Hotel Security

I moved to the hotel phone and dialed the operator, then asked to be connected to my airline. I met with a recording that acknowledged an unusually long hold time and issued a blanket apology to callers concerned with missing luggage. I held for a half a minute more, then hung up.

Within seconds, the phone rang. "Hello?" I answered.

"Is this Ms. Night in room 319?" said a male voice.

I slammed the phone onto the receiver before contemplating my very actions confirmed who I was. Before the phone could ring again, I called the front desk.

"This is Madison Night. Would it be possible for me to change rooms?"

"Is there a problem with your room?" asked Harrison. "You requested a view and we think you have one of the most spectacular that we have to offer."

"I know, yes, that's true." I looked at the crutches lying across the bed. "I was wondering if you had anything closer to the first floor. I didn't expect to have such trouble with the crutches."

"Would you like to use our hotel wheelchair?"

"No!" I answered quickly. "Is there a Jack Jordan who works for the hotel?"

"Yes," he paused. "He's our security manager. Ms. Night, are you sure there's no problem?"

"Can you ask Mr. Jordan to meet me in the bar at nine o'clock this evening?"

"Mr. Jordan is not in the habit of meeting guests for drinks."

"Tell him—tell him I've been hired to investigate this hotel. Tell him Ms. Day asked me to meet with him."

The concierge's voice dropped to whisper. "Ms. Day arranged this?"

"Yes," I lied.

"I'll deliver the message."

I hung up the phone. Now what? I'd demanded a meeting with the head of security, who I didn't know, who wouldn't recognize me. Or maybe he would. Maybe he was one of the voices from the balcony above me. Maybe he was planning to grab me. Maybe I'd just organized a meeting with the man who I wanted to avoid.

Or maybe I was going crazy.

It was after seven and I was still in the hotel bathrobe. I had nothing to wear except for the vintage blue and white double-knit polyester dress and jacket I'd worn on the plane, and even though I was most comfortable in my sixties vintage attire, right now, that outfit felt too conspicuous. I looked at the suitcase sitting on the luggage cart. No, those were someone else's things. I wouldn't want a stranger rooting around through my things, and I was willing to bet the obsessive-compulsive who had packed three different sizes of hand sanitizer in separate Ziploc baggies wanted it even less.

I redressed in my sheath dress and used the hotel hair drier to fluff my short blond hair into its normal bubble style, draped my small handbag over my shoulder, and left with the crutches digging into my underarms.

Two blocks from the hotel I found a souvenir store. I bought two packs of cotton panties, an elastic bandage, and a navy blue sweatshirt with Carmel embroidered across the chest in gold and white thread. I asked the saleslady to cut the tags from the sweatshirt so I could put it on immediately. I added a pair of sunglasses from the display rack, a travel-sized tube of Motrin, and a pink lip-gloss, paid, and left. The short man from the elevator stood in front of the store, his back to me.

"I don't know if she arrived or not. She was due today, but there was some kind of mix-up in Dallas," he said into a cell phone.

A shiver ran down my spine despite the warmth of the sweatshirt. The man turned around and saw me, then smiled and pulled his phone away from his head.

"Hey, it's the pretty little blonde from the elevators. You find your room okay?" he asked.

"Yes, I did."

"That's too bad. My friend and I were trying to figure out which one of us would have the honor of helping you." He reached out and grabbed for my plastic shopping bag. "But my friend isn't here now, so I guess the honor's all mine. Call me Louis."

"I'm not done shopping yet," I said instead of offering a return introduction. I held the bag even though he tried to pull it from my grasp.

"Maybe you're not, but the stores are. It's closing time around here."

I looked behind me. On the other side of the window, the clerk turned the Open sign to Closed. The lights were out in the store next to them. I tugged on the shopping bag, trying to break it free from his grasp. One of the handles broke. The bag dropped and split, my personal items spilling onto the sidewalk around the feet of people swirling around us.

Louis stared at the oversized sunglasses, anti-inflammatories, and cotton panties. He made no move to pick any of it up. Slowly, he looked up at me. His cheeks were taut, his lips drawn.

I couldn't read his eyes because they were hidden behind his own pair of sunglasses, but I imagined they weren't smiling.

"Kind of suspicious, taking a getaway and not packing your essentials. By the looks of it, you didn't plan on this vacation."

"Is this man bothering you?" said another man, approaching us.

It took me a second to recognize Harrison the Concierge without his hotel uniform, but when I did, I could have hugged him if it wouldn't have included falling off the crutches.

Louis backed away from us and held his hands in the air. "I was just offering to help, that's all." Before either one of us could say another word he turned around and disappeared into the crowd of swirling people.

FOUR

Harrison corralled my purchases, hugged them to his chest, and stood. I leaned on the crutches and reached for the items, but he took the torn bag from me instead, loaded everything back inside, and knotted the handles together.

"Are you okay?" he asked.

"I'm fine. I didn't expect that man to—to—"

I didn't know what it was I'd expected or not expected from the man who called himself Louis. I didn't know how to explain to Harrison that I'd overheard very strange things. And I didn't know how to rationalize, to myself, that little by little, I was losing touch with reality.

"You seem a little shaken up. Would you like me to walk you back to the hotel?" Harrison asked.

I scanned the street, looking for signs of Louis, but there were none. I didn't know where he had gone. I wanted to take Harrison up on his offer, but I didn't know how to explain my paranoia without looking like a fool.

"Only if I can buy you a drink to say thank you."

Harrison looked surprised. "I thought you wanted to have a drink with our security manager?"

"Yes, that's true."

I thought for a moment and bit my lip. "I'm sorry. Is there another way I can say thank you?"

He blushed, and then I blushed, realizing how the whole thing had sounded. First I'd come off like I was trying to fill my happy hour dance card, and now I sounded like a cougar on vacation.

We walked to the hotel side by side, me on the crutches and Harrison holding my bag. I wanted nothing more than to throw the crutches away, to burn them, to wake up tomorrow morning and be able to walk like I walked before the skiing accident, but the voice of the hospital doctor echoed in my head. *Recovery will take time. Don't try to rush it.*

We reached the hotel quickly. I leveraged my weight against the banister and hopped up the three steps in front of the hotel door. I turned to face Harrison and looped my hand through the handle of the shopping bag.

"Thank you," I said. "I'm sorry I already made other arrangements for tonight."

"Tell you what. I'll come to the bar around nine. If you're alone, I'll join you. If you're with Mr. Jordan, I won't."

"That hardly seems fair. You're helping me and now I'm inconveniencing you."

"Ms. Night, I'm happy to help you. In fact, if there's anything you need, anything you forgot to buy at that drug store, I want you to call me." He pulled a small notepad out of his jacket pocket and wrote a phone number on a blank piece of paper, then tore it off and handed it to me.

"Does the hotel offer this kind of service to every guest?" I asked.

He leaned in and whispered, "Only the ones who know Ms. Day." When he pulled back, he smiled a warm smile.

It was well after eight by the time I returned to my room. I hadn't seen any other familiar faces in the lobby or hallway, and I hoped the opposite was true as well. In less than an hour I'd be sitting with the hotel security manager and I'd be able to tell him about the conversation I'd over-heard. If he believed me, I'd tell him about the men by the elevators. Harrison could verify one of the guests had approached me on the street. I felt better knowing I was doing something about the situation, versus locking myself in my room and fearing for the worst. The only thing I did fear was being recognized. Walking around in a vintage dress with a sixties-style blond bubble cut wasn't doing me any favors in the anonymity category, and my one attempt to blend in, in the Carmel sweatshirt, had already been made. I needed some kind of disguise, but aside from wearing the hotel bathrobe, I had no other options.

Unless…the suitcase. Maybe there was something in the suitcase.

I flipped it open and dug past the layer of Ziploc bag-gies to the neat piles of folded clothes. I set the baggies on the bed, exposing a red and white bandana print and a cow-boy hat. What the—?

I closed the suitcase and located a luggage tag right next to the white tag the airline had wrapped around the handle. "Elliott Lisbon" read the name. Elliott. This was one odd dude. What kind of a weekend did he think he was taking? A country and western escape?

I moved the cowboy hat to the side and picked up the red and white bandana print. It was a long prairie skirt, the kind I passed over in countless thrift shops while I looked for the sixties vintage I favored, only, this one had tags attached.

Was Elliott a cross-dresser? I put the skirt back into the suitcase and rooted further down. A red and white poppy print
peeked out from below something chambray. It was a swing
dress with dark brown accents. I could wear that, I supposed.
Whoever this Elliott character was, he was nothing like me,
and that might work to my advantage.

I changed into a clean pair of panties and pulled the
swing dress over my head. It was pretty in a sundress kind of
way. Repeated washings would soften the fabric, but like the
bandana skirt, this dress had tags on it, too. I imagined Elliott
shopping for this weekend with the same care with which he
had packed his toiletries. I imagined, for a second, the
stranger's reaction when he opened my suitcase and saw my
polyester dresses and four tubes of sunscreen. I was sure it
would be a letdown.

I fished the elastic bandage out of the bag from the
drug store and wound it around my knee, tight enough to
minimize the swelling but not so tight I cut off my circula-
tion. I swallowed four anti-inflammatories with a glass of water from the sink and looked at my reflection.

Exhaustion painted the two dark circles under my eyes.
I needed to sleep tonight. The time change, going from the
east coast to the west coast, had left me feeling like it was going on midnight, not nine. And being a morning person, I
wasn't used to being up until midnight. I'd make my meeting
with Mr. Jordan brief. I'd tell him what was going on and I'd
retire.

I ran cool water into my hands and ran my hands
through my hair, then massaged a dollop of complimentary
hotel moisturizer into it and combed it straight back. My lips
were rosy, as were my cheeks. As the clock approached nine,

I thrust my room key into my handbag, grabbed the crutches, and headed down to the bar.

I took a seat along the wall next to the fireplace and looked for familiar faces. I saw none. A cocktail waitress approached me and I ordered a glass of white wine. As she left to fill my order, I saw my worst nightmare, standing in the entranceway. The two men from the elevator, engrossed in a heated conversation with Harrison the Concierge. With them was a fourth person, and there was no mistaking his identity.

It was my Ex, Brad Turlington.

FIVE

Brad had followed me from Pennsylvania. My paranoia had been on target.

I slouched down in my chair and watched the scene. From my vantage point, which was across a crowded room where people and pets mingled over wine and cheese, I knew I wouldn't hear their conversation, so I listened to their body language. From what it was telling me, these four men were arguing.

Harrison was doing the talking and the other men were listening. His gestures, though kept close to his body, were emphatic.

Louis was red in the face. He didn't like what he was being told.

And then there was Brad. He wore a straw Hamburg tipped down low over his forehead. His wavy black hair peeked out in the back. He stood inches over the other men, his white zip front GE nylon windbreaker open over an orange and white checkered shirt. His hands were in the pockets of his khaki trousers, and the sunlight gleamed off of the face of his 1960's Rolex Submariner watch. I knew the watch. I'd given it to him for Christmas less than a year ago.

I felt sick. My heart raced and I shifted to the side, to remain in the shadow of the fireplace. It couldn't be, it couldn't be! I was trapped in a nightmare of past and present. I wanted to leave but standing up and fussing with the crutches would only draw attention to me, attention I couldn't afford.

The fourth man, the one in the suit, had his arms crossed over his chest. His attention was so focused on Harrison's face he didn't notice the small dog sniffing his shoe. Suddenly, as if startled, he kicked his foot out with a jerk. The dog jumped backward. A woman in a navy blue dress scooped up the dog and glared at the man. After he apologized to her, his eyes swept the room. I lowered my head and slunk down further.

A cocktail waitress came around to check on different tables and, when she got close enough to block my view of the men, I waved her over.

"Hi, I'm supposed to be meeting someone here, but I need to leave," I whispered. "Would it be possible to leave a message with you?"

"Sure," she said, her hand fishing through the pocket of a faded blue floral apron tied around her waist.

She handed me a ballpoint pen and a blank order ticket. Hastily I scribbled on it. *Mr. Jordan. I couldn't wait. Please meet me tomorrow morning for breakfast. Madison Night (room 319).* I folded the paper and wrote "Jack Jordan, Hotel Security" on the more blank of the two sides of the paper. I held it out to her and she took it.

"Are you okay? You look like you saw a ghost."

"Worse than a ghost, I think. Is there a way out of here other than the entrance past the bar?"

She looked over her shoulder. I followed her gaze. The men were gone and I didn't know which direction they'd headed.

"There's the service elevator off the kitchen, but I can't let you take it."

"Please," I said. I reached out and put my hand on her forearm. She looked at it, then back at me.

"Are you sure you're okay?" she asked again.

My mind scrambled for something to say without sounding crazy. "I'm sorry. I'm on a bit of medication from an injury last week and I feel woozy. I should get back to my room."

"Let me get someone from the hotel to escort you back to your room."

"Wait, do you have a wheelchair?" I asked.

"Yes."

Before I could stop her, she left.

I knew I wasn't woozy from medication. Aside from the jetlag, my mind was clear. I looked around the room again and picked out Louis, Brad, and Grey Suit at the bar, their backs to me. I wasn't sure where Harrison the Concierge had gone, but this was as good a chance as any for me to get out of there. I stood up and reached for the crutches, then headed past the other guests toward the kitchen. A collapsible wheelchair sat against the wall. I looked through the glass on one of the doors and saw the cocktail waitress talking to Harrison.

I put my head down and left the way I'd come. I reached my room undetected. I threw the crutches on the carpet and sat on the bed. I needed to talk to someone. I needed to find out what was going on. I needed an ally.

I dialed the operator. "Hello, this is Madison Night in room 319. I'm trying to reach Jack Jordan from hotel security. Is there a way to reach him?"

"Hold for a moment and I'll ring the concierge desk," she said politely.

"No!" I answered quickly. "Please don't. Is there a way to get a message to him directly, without involving anyone else from the hotel?"

"I can page him to call me. What would you like the message to be?"

"Tell him I'm sorry I had to cancel—no. Tell him I need to see him—no, not that either. Can you tell him to call me?" I held my breath, knowing how I sounded. "It's in regards to an issue with the hotel."

"Ms. Night, if your room is somehow unsatisfactory, I can try to make different arrangements for you."

"No, that's not it. There's something going on tonight he needs to know about."

"Ms. Night, are you in some kind of trouble?" she asked.

"Please page Mr. Jordan. I'll be in my room waiting for his call."

My knee throbbed. I leaned back on my tush and spun until I was long ways on the bed. My foot kicked the suitcase balanced on the luggage rack by the end, and the case tipped over, spilling the contents onto the floor. On top of everything else, I knew the cross-dressing germophobe would have serious issues knowing his stuff had been in contact with hotel-grade carpet. But now that the contents had been spilled onto the floor, there was no way to pack it back the way it had been packed. Which meant, I might as well take advantage of the opportunity to see if there was anything in there I could use.

I slid off the bedspread and eased myself onto the floor next to a pile of Ziploc baggies. I piled them back inside the suitcase and found an envelope protruding from an interior pocket. I slipped the envelope out and read the name that had been caligraphied across the heavy weight paper: *Ms. Elli Lisbon.*

My cross-dressing germophobe was a woman.

Temporarily distracted from far bigger problems, I rooted through the clothes on the floor. Under the red bandana printed maxi-skirt was a white tee with a tiny pocket. Under that was a red canvas bucket hat, red canvas ballerina flats three sizes bigger than my own foot size, and a red and white striped canvas purse. Other outfits were similarly packed: a blue and brown sleeveless sundress with chambray flip flops and an oversized crushable straw hat.

I slid the card from the envelope and read the invitation. *Kick up your heels at the Annual Cattle Baron's Ball!* Said the headline, printed in deep red ink on thick stationery. I glanced back at the bucket hat and the chambray flip flops. Maybe ball meant something different in Texas.

But then, it struck me that Ms. Elli Lisbon and her assortment of weird western clothes might get me out of there safely.

I struggled to my feet, then pushed the western wear aside and traded the poppy printed dress for the prairie skirt. It hung to the floor, perfect for hiding my injured knee and battered white Keds. I pulled on her blue Dodgers t-shirt, then picked up the blue Carmel sweatshirt I'd bought hours earlier and tore it along a seam until I had a square of fabric to tie over my short hair, babushka style. I wasn't concerned with looking stylish or retro or fashionable. My only concern was with not looking like me.

I moved to the hallway and pulled the bathroom door closed to see my reflection. If success could be measured by impromptu Halloween-like attire, it had been achieved. And if I was wrong, I had a good start on an insanity case.

The phone rang. I picked up the extension in the bathroom. Necessity in the form of knee pain forced me to close the toilet and sit on the lid. This was not my proudest moment.

"Hello?"

"Ms. Night? This is Jack Jordan."

"Mr. Jordan—" I started.

"Call me Jack."

"Jack, I'm sorry I had to cancel our meeting tonight. Something came up—I mean, something happened. Something that concerns the hotel."

"Ms. Night—" he started.

"Call me Madison," I said.

"Madison, were you in the hotel bar earlier this evening?"

"Yes, but I had to leave. There are men who followed me here from Dallas. I don't know what they want from me."

"How do you know they followed you?"

"I overheard them. They knew I came in from Dallas. They knew I started my trip on the east coast. One of your hotel members is involved with them. I didn't realize it at first. I was shopping, and when I left the store one of these men was outside waiting for me. I think he was going to force me to go with him, but your hotel concierge appeared and helped me. He walked me back to the hotel and I thought I was safe, until I saw him talking to the men at the bar, so I think he's involved too."

The other end of the phone was silent, and I wondered if Jack Jordan of hotel security was still on the line. "Hello?"

"I'm here, Ms. Ni—Madison. Is that all you want to tell me?"

I wanted to pretend I'd told him everything, but deep down, I knew there was more. "There's another man here, too. Brad Turlington. He and I had a relationship that ended abruptly. I don't know how he knew I was coming here, but he found out and followed me. Mr. Jord—Jack, I do not want to see that man."

"The best way for you to not see that man is to remain in your room, at least for the rest of the night. Can you do that?"

"Yes."

"I'm going to see what I can find out. In the meantime, is there anything I can arrange for you? Have you had dinner?"

"I'm not hungry."

"The kitchen stays open for room service until eleven, so you have a little time if you change your mind."

"Thank you."

After I hung up the phone, I changed out of the makeshift undercover outfit and took another shower, then pulled on a fresh pair of panties and a nightshirt I'd bought at the drug store and crawled into bed. Twenty minutes later I called room service and ordered a Cobb Salad.

I pulled on a pair of white linen pants from Elli's suitcase and refolded the clothes that had fallen onto the floor.

The hotel was eerily silent, except for footsteps over my head. The men who occupied that room, who I'd heard talking on the balcony, were moving about. I crossed the carpet and unlocked the balcony doors a crack and listened. Any conversation I might have heard was drowned by the sound of the water crashing on the rocks of Monterey.

I unscrewed the cap from a bottle of sparkling water from the mini fridge. I poured half of it into a plastic cup from the bathroom, settling into the plush armchair next to the sliding glass doors. There was a knock on the door to my room.

"Ms. Night? It's Jack Jordan. I have your room service," said a deep voice.

I set the water on the table and crossed the room to the door. "Just a minute." I hadn't expected the head of security to deliver my food, but, in light of the circumstances, I didn't mind the extra attention. As I reached for the chain that locked the door, I peeked through the peephole and froze.

Jack Jordan, head of security wasn't standing in front of my door.

Harrison the Concierge was. And there was no tray of room service in sight.

SIX

I'd undone the chain, and now my fingers fumbled with it, trying to get it back into place. There was no point in pretending I wasn't in the room. I backed away, stumbling when I connected with the corner of the mattress. With my hands on the surface of the muted turquoise and yellow floral coverlet, I guided myself around the bed to the phone and dialed the operator.

"Yes, Ms. Night?" she answered. For a split second I was spooked by the fact that she knew who was calling.

"Can you please page Jack Jordan again?" I asked in a low whisper.

"Didn't he call you earlier?"

"Yes, but I need to speak to him again."

"Ms. Night, are you okay?"

"There's a man at my door. He's trying to get to me. I'm trapped inside and I need help," I hissed.

"Ms. Night—"

"Hurry!" I said.

I hung up the phone and turned around. There was a click by the door, the slip of a key sliding into the slot. He was coming in after me. I moved past the second of the beds to the curtains by the balcony, my hands searching for the opening. My room was on the third floor, too high for me to jump. The front door opened. I slid the balcony door open further. Harrison entered the room. His eyes went wide as he saw me move through the narrow opening.

"Madison!" he cried out.

I stumbled backward, over the chair I'd rested in earlier, contorted my body and lunged toward the metal railing. Strong arms closed around me from behind, pinning my own arms along the sides of my body. I pushed my head back hard, clunking my skull against his forehead.

"Ow!" he said. He dropped his arms from around my chest to around my waist and picked me up, then carried me back into the room. With his foot he pushed the balcony doors shut, still holding me. I planted my feet on the side of the bed and pushed backward, but with the doors shut, I only succeeded in pushing him up against the glass.

"Shhhhh. Madison, Ms. Night. Calm down. I'm Jack Jordan. Shhh. I'm hotel security. Shhh, shhh. Let me explain."

I had little energy left, little enough that I needed time to rest if I intended to escape. I went limp. He put his hands on my upper arms and turned me around, then lowered me onto the bed. I looked up at him. He reached behind him to the arm chair and pulled it forward, then sat down directly across from me. Before he spoke, he pulled out his wallet and opened it to a pair of identification cards that showed out from under plastic windows. He held the wallet toward me and I took it.

The first card was a driver's license for Jack Jordan. The address was in Carmel By-The-Sea, California. The other card was hotel identification. Again I read his name, next to the title of Hotel Security Manager. Both pictures were of the same man, the man with salt and pepper hair who in front of me. I handed the wallet back.

"I don't understand," I said.

"Your message to me—you were right. There's something going on at the hotel and I'm investigating it. I needed a way to keep tabs on them so I've been standing in as the hotel concierge. People trust the concierge. People don't trust hotel security."

"So when I checked in, you were undercover?"

"In a manner of speaking. The real concierge has been around at all times, ready to step in and help if need be."

"And outside of the souvenir store, earlier today? How did you happen to be there when I needed you?"

"I've been trying to understand their operation. When you said you had the wrong suitcase, I suspected you might be working with them. I followed you to see where you'd go, what you'd do. Your reaction to Louis made it clear you didn't know him."

"I can't shake the feeling he wanted something from me, I just don't know what."

"You're a noticeable woman, Madison, with your fluffy blond hair and aqua outfit. Even in a town filled with tourists, it's not that strange Louis remembered you from your meeting by the elevator. Add in the crutches, and, well, let's just say you're not going to fly under the radar. He probably picked you out of the crowd just like I did. If you look like you look, especially in a town with Doris Day history, you're going to get noticed. It's likely he just wanted to talk to a pretty lady."

"And you—you were the concierge. The letter you sent to my room was signed Jack Jordan. That's why I asked to meet you for a drink."

"The letter was for real. You suspected we had a foul-up. I had to make sure we didn't, otherwise it would raise questions about how we were running the hotel. Turns out the foul up was in Dallas."

"Dallas…" I said slowly. "That's why I thought the men were after me. I heard them say 'she's coming in from Dallas.' I thought they meant me." I paused. "So who did they mean?"

"Are you traveling with something valuable?" he asked.

"Right now I'm traveling with little more than the clothes I'm wearing and they aren't even mine."

"But in your real suitcase, was there something in there with a high value?"

I thought for a moment about the double-knit polyester outfits I'd packed, the four tubes of sunscreen, the assortment of Keds, and the collapsible straw hat to keep me shielded from the sun. I seriously doubted the whole lot would be worth over a couple hundred dollars, tops. Before I could answer, Jack continued.

"I have reason to believe they're expecting a package that was routed through Dallas, something that might've been on your flight. There's a good chance their package never arrived or went to someone else, just like your suitcase did."

"But they knew I stopped in Dallas on my way from the east coast."

Jack scratched his head, his salt-and-pepper hair mussed up. "Madison, I don't think the east coast they mentioned is the one you came from."

"I don't understand."

"Those men weren't talking about you. They're talking about the east Barbary Coast."

"Africa?"

He nodded. "You said they called it 'she'?"

"Yes, that's why I thought they meant me."

"Madison, they're not here to pick up you. I think they're here to pick up an extremely rare rough cut diamond."

SEVEN

"And what about the other man? How is he involved?" I asked tentatively.

"That's where I'm stumped. I ran the name you gave me, 'Brad Turlington,' through the hotel reservations and there's no record of him."

"You were talking to him at the bar while I was waiting. It was you, and him and two other guys. You were arguing."

"I was at the bar, yes. A couple of guys were talking baseball. Things got heated. Those two guys know me as the concierge. As long as I'm here, I have to treat every person who I see like a guest, for the sake of the hotel. Are you sure you didn't make a mistake?"

I had been sure. As sure as I'd been the man sitting in front of me was involved in something crooked, as sure as I'd been the men above me were out to kidnap me. I'd been as sure as when I'd thought I had the suitcase of a cross-dresser from Dallas, and as sure as I'd been months ago when I thought I had everything I'd ever needed out of life.

I wanted to believe I hadn't seen Brad. I wanted to believe I'd left him behind when I left Pennsylvania, that I'd moved on.

"Madison, look at me."

I looked up from my hands to the face of the security manager. The sun had etched lines of maturity into his face, but his ruddy complexion lent him a youthful appearance.

"Madison, why did you react the way you did? When I came into your room. Like you were fighting for your life?"

"Because I am," I said. I stared behind him at the bright white baseboard that joined the textured wheat wallpaper to the muted tones of the carpet. A soft ivory, or better yet, a taupe would have been better complement to the décor.

I shut my eyes, blocking out the decorator's instinct to improve the room and thought about my actions. When I opened my eyes, I looked Jack in the eyes.

"This trip was meant as a way for me to get away from what's going on in my life right now." Or not going on, as the case may be. "I need a fresh start, but before I can look forward I have to shake this feeling that another shoe is about to drop."

"You had a bad scare. Anybody would have reacted the way you did. I'm going to keep looking out for you because that's my job, but I have to tell you I don't know anything about this third man. As far as I can tell, there's only the two of them, and nobody followed you here, from Dallas or from Pennsylvania. Can you believe that?"

"I guess I have to."

"I think you should stay in for the rest of the night," he said.

"I will. Wait, where's my dinner?"

"What dinner?"

"I called for room service. You even said you had it. Before I opened the door."

"I did, didn't I?" he turned around and looked at the door, then scratched his head. "After we talked, I asked the front desk and the operator to let me know if you made or received any calls. They told me you called in a dinner order. I figured you might freak out when you saw who I was, so I used that to get you to the door."

"So where's my food?"

"They didn't have an order. I figured you changed your mind." He looked at the clock behind him. "But it's late, the kitchen's closed now. I don't know what happened to your food, but how about I get you something from town? You like pizza?"

"You don't have to do that," I said, only half-meaning it.

"Then let the hotel pick up your breakfast tomorrow morning. Give your name to the restaurant hostess and she'll take care of the bill."

"Thank you, Jack."

"Are you going to be okay by yourself?"

"You don't happen to keep spare pets around the hotel, do you?" I asked.

"You know, it's not a bad idea. Maybe I should suggest it to Ms. Day." He smiled warmly.

I stood and walked him to the door.

"Good night, Madison. Try to get some sleep. I'll check on you tomorrow."

He opened the door to my room and stepped into the hallway, nearly tripping over a room service tray on the carpet in front of the door.

"What the—?"

"I didn't hear a knock. Did you hear a knock?" I asked.

His face clouded. "No, I didn't hear a knock." He bent down and picked up the tray, then carried it past me into the room. "Where do you want it?"

"Bed's fine."

He set the tray on the bed. A silver dome covered a plate that sat on the center of a white doily-like mat. Tucked under the plate was a white envelope. Jack picked up the envelope, tapped it twice on the edge of the tray, and held it up. "Dinner's on me."

"I ordered a lot of food. You might want to look at the bill before you make that kind of offer."

He raised an eyebrow then made a showing of peeking into the envelope. Within moments the humor left his face, replaced with a creased forehead and a downturned mouth.

"I was kidding. I ordered a Cobb Salad. How much could that be?" I asked, straining forward to see the bill.

He looked up and stared at me for an uncomfortable amount of time.

"Jack? What is it?"

"Nothing." He slid the envelope into the back pocket of his pants. "Stay put tonight, Madison. And make sure you lock the door."

An uneasiness swept over me, like the chill that shudders through your body seconds after biting into ice. I started to shut the door and the phone rang. Before the latch connected on the door, Jack pushed back inside.

"Does anybody know your room number?" he asked.

"I don't think so."

"Then pick up the receiver. but don't say anything."

The shrill ringing continued in the background. "Won't it be better to let it ring?"

"No."

On his instructions, I picked up the receiver and held it to my head. The line crackled. Jack stood next to me, and I angled the device so it pointed to the ceiling, so we both had a chance at hearing. He held a finger up to his mouth to remind me to be quiet.

"That wasn't very bright, skipping out on us tonight," said a male voice. "Don't try to hide. We're watching you." The line cracked a bit more, and then there was a click.

"They know I was at the bar, that I saw them and left. I don't like this," I said.

"I don't think that message was for you." Jack dialed zero on the phone and spoke into the receiver. "Hi Sophie, this is Mr. Jordan. A call came in to 319 just now. What can you tell me about it?"

I heard a tinny voice through the receiver, picking out only the occasional word. "Ms. Night wants privacy for the rest of the night. If anybody rings her room, either get a message or forward it to my room. Is that clear?"

He hung up the receiver. "Madison, I don't know what to tell you. Our operator asked someone to cover the booth while she stepped out for a break so she doesn't know anything about the call—if it came from inside the hotel our outside. I know you're worried, but you won't be interrupted again. Can I do anything else to make you more comfortable?"

"I don't suppose you'd be willing to share a room with me tonight, would you?" I said, not quite believing the words coming out of my mouth. Too many unexpected things had happened since I'd arrived in Carmel, and I didn't want to be alone. "There are two beds, after all." I felt my face go hot.

"I'm sorry, I shouldn't have asked. I don't know what came over me," I added.

He blushed. "It's okay. Under the circumstances, I'm surprised it took so long for you to ask. And even though I can appreciate the request, I have to decline. There's someone at home waiting for me."

This time the blush crept over my face, and didn't leave until well after I locked the door behind him.

After Jack left, I wandered to the room service tray and looked under the silver dome. My appetite was no longer an issue. I put the dome back on top of the plate and moved it back into the hall, then hung the Do Not Disturb sign on the door and put the chain in place. I changed out of the maxi skirt and crawled into the bed in my underwear.

I awoke in the middle of the night. The room was a cocoon of darkness and the only sound was that of pacing over my head. Someone above me was very much awake. The clock read three-thirty. There were too many hours between now and dawn for me to consider anything other than staying put safely under the covers.

I thought about what Jack had said earlier. He checked out the people I thought I'd seen, and Brad hadn't been one of them. Was it possible I was so desperate to believe he'd follow me that I was seeing him in places where he wasn't? And if so, how long until the memory of him faded and I could go on with my life, life as Madison Night, single forty-something? I'd heard statistics about single women in their forties, statistics more in favor of lightning striking than finding a relationship. I didn't want a relationship anymore. I'd figure out a way to get everything I wanted out of life and I'd do it all for me. Who knows? When I figured out where I wanted to live, maybe I'd even get a dog.

The footsteps over my head continued in a random cycle. I pictured someone crossing the room, stopping to look out the window, then crossing back. That's it, I realized. Whatever it is they're looking for out their window, maybe I'll see it, too. I pushed the covers back and eased myself onto the floor, then quietly hobbled to the curtains and the magnificent view I'd been ignoring.

Earlier, before I'd considered that there was a threat to my presence, I'd stood on the balcony and stared at the view. The dark blue water had crashed against the rocky Monterey cliffs in the distance while the sun cast shimmering highlights over the beach, the sand, the horizon, and the ocean. But now, in the middle of the night, I saw none of that. What I saw was a flickering light, flashing at equally repeated intervals, from the sidewalk half a block from the hotel. Flash-Flash-Flash. Pause. Flash Flash Flash. Pause. I strained my eyes to make out the figure with the light, but I couldn't. Aside from the light, there was nothing decipherable about the scene.

The phone jangled a tortured ring. I jumped. My heart pounded in my chest and adrenaline shot through my arms and legs. I stared at the machine on the table between the beds. Jack had given instructions not to allow any calls into my room. Was this a call for me that had been screened?

I gripped the long curtains and stared at the phone, wishing for a sign. After twelve rings, the phone stopped. I crawled across the bed, closer to the windows, and sat next to the phone, waiting. When it started ringing a second time, I was equally scared. I picked up the receiver after one ring and held it to my head, not saying a word.

"You saw the signal. Now it's time for us to see the pretty lady," said a low voice. "You have fifteen minutes." The line disconnected.

I didn't know how to reach Jack. I sat on the bed, considering my options for about forty-five seconds. When nothing else came to mind, I dialed the operator.

"Good evening, Ms. Night," said a female voice.

"Hi, is there a way to get a message to Mr. Jordan?" I asked in a hushed voice. I kept one hand cupped around the receiver so my voice wouldn't carry.

"Ms. Night? I think there's a problem with our connection. I can barely hear you," said the woman.

I cleared my throat. "Mr. Jordan left instructions for you to keep calls from coming through to my room, but one just did. I need to talk to him to tell him what the caller said. I know it's late, but is there a way to reach him? An emergency number?"

"Ms. Night, Mr. Jordan gave me no such instruction."

"Yes he did. I was sitting right next to him when he told you."

"I'm sorry, Ms. Night, but I don't know what you're talking about. Jack Jordan left no such instruction. In fact, I haven't spoken to Mr. Jordan since he returned from his vacation last week."

EIGHT

"Is this Sophie?"

"Sophie who?"

"Sophie the operator. Mr. Jordan called the operator 'Sophie' earlier."

"Ms. Night, we don't have an operator named Sophie. Are you okay?"

"No, I'm not. I'm coming to the lobby."

"Ms. Night—" the operator started, but I set the receiver back into the cradle before letting her finish her thought.

It was a few minutes after four. The sun wouldn't be up for another hour or so, but I wasn't comfortable staying in my room. Something was happening, something that had to do with me, and I wasn't going to stick around to let it happen. I knew my injured knee would hinder any chance of leaving the hotel, but the idea of staying was worse than that of trying to get away.

I wrapped my knee, redressed in the maxi skirt, and pulled the Dodgers t-shirt over my head. I slicked my hair back with hotel moisturizer, stepped back into my sneakers, grabbed my crutches, and locked the door behind me.

The hallways were empty. I winced every time the crutches made a sound, but made it to the elevators and traveled down to the ground level. It took longer than I'd thought to move to the lobby of the hotel. I hid behind a column and leaned forward, looking at the concierge desk. The first place I'd seen Jack Jordan had been at that concierge desk and I hoped, desperately, he wasn't there again. A woman in a white shirt, thin black neck tie, and black blazer stood behind the desk tapping keys on the hidden keyboard. Her hair was parted on the side and slicked back into a tight bun she wore at the nape of her neck. Her nametag said Kitty. Other than a thick coat of scarlet red color on her lips, her face appeared un-made-up.

Slowly, I approached her.

She looked up and smiled.

"Good morning," she said in a cheerful voice. "Or at least it will be morning soon, I guess."

"Good morning. Can you tell me what time the sun comes up?"

"Yes I can," she said with a smile. She waited a beat for me to acknowledge that technically she'd answered my question, but I wasn't in the mood for jokes.

"What time?" I prompted.

She leaned forward over the surface of the concierge desk and looked at the door, then pulled herself back and looked at her watch. "You'll see a glow in about ten minutes. Everything turns kind of an orangey-gold. You'll see the sun shortly after that, maybe fifteen, maybe twenty minutes. In forty-five it'll will be hard for our guests to sleep if they didn't shut their curtains."

"Thank you," I said, starting toward the door.

"It's still pretty dark out. Would you like a flashlight?"

I turned back to her, poised atop the crutches. "I don't know if I can maneuver these and hold a flashlight, too."

"Where are you going?"

"I'm an early bird. I thought I'd go to the beach, sit on one of the rocks by the road, and listen to the waves."

"I broke my leg last year and was on crutches for a solid three months. It's a bitch getting down the slope of Ocean Avenue with them. Hold on."

She disappeared behind a door to the left of her. I tapped my fingers on the marble counter, eager for her to return. I didn't know what kind of time I had but I didn't think I had much.

From farther inside the hotel I heard a soft ding. The elevator. I quickly grabbed the crutches and moved to a yellow gingham sofa. I propped the crutches behind another column, out of sight. I reclined, pulling the fabric of the maxi skirt around my legs. I rolled into the back of the sofa and hoped I looked like someone who had chosen not to sleep in their room.

"Where is she?" asked a familiar voice. It was same man who had cornered me in front of the drug store before Jack Jordan had come to my rescue, before Jack Jordan turned out to be not who he'd seemed. It was Louis.

"She was here a second ago," said Kitty.

I curled back into a ball on the sofa but kept my head raised so I could hear their conversation.

"Did you see which way she went?"

An awkward silence followed. My mind pictured a thousand permutations of what was going on. I imagined the man seeing the crutches I'd stashed behind the column and coming over to me, to do—do do what I didn't know, only, I was convinced it wasn't going to be good.

"She said she was going to the ocean."

"At this hour?" Louis asked. "Sounds suspicious."

"That's what I thought. I said I was getting her a flashlight but she must have left without it."

"Tell you what, Kitty, I'll look for her. The ocean, you said?"

"That's what she said."

I waited on the sofa, considering my options. I could go back to my room, or I could follow Louis, the man from the elevators. After the front door to the hotel shut, I stood and flexed my legs individually, then spied a small flat rectangle on the lobby floor. A room key tucked into a paper sleeve. I felt my pockets for my own key. It was where I'd tucked it, in the pocket of the skirt.

I bent down to pick up the keycard when Kitty called out to me. "There you are!"

"I had to go back to my room for something, but I must have dropped my key." I flipped the sleeve over. The number 419 was written on the back. I looked at the front doors, then quickly looked back down at the keycard. Louis had dropped this.

"Looks like the sun is starting to come up. I won't need that flashlight after all." A cloudy plan formed in my mind. I made a show of fussing with my crutches and hobbling out the front door, then tossed them by the flower beds that decorated the walk up entrance to the hotel. Adrenaline coursed through my body and eliminated any pain that had been there days earlier. In the dark, I moved to the side of the hotel and reentered through another door.

I picked up the receiver on the hotel phone that sat next to the ugly lamp on the marble table across from the elevators. I dialed 419. I counted at least ten rings, a good indication that the room was empty. With one hand on the wall, I moved through the hallway to the elevator, then hit the button for the third floor. A plan had formed, but first I needed to better my disguise.

In my room, I emptied a packet of instant coffee into a hotel glass and added enough of the serum from Elli Lisbon's overnight kit to make a paste with my fingers. I raked the resulting brown glop through my hair, temporarily turning myself from a blonde to a brunette. Next I swept my face generously with bronzer, then changed from the bandana printed skirt into a pair of white linen drawstring-waist pants, the faded Dodgers t-shirt, and a dark brown cowboy hat. I looked at myself one last time and was shocked by the stranger in the mirror.

I dialed 419 and heard the ringing phone through the ceiling. Five rings, then six, then seven. When I hit double digits, I knew no one would answer. I left the room and returned to the elevator, riding up one floor. I followed the same path I'd been following to get to my room one floor below, took three quick breaths to pump up my courage, and shoved the keycard into the door. I held my own key in the opposite hand, prepared with a cover story if anyone were to discover me. Nobody did.

The light outside the door turned to a bright lime green. Quietly, I turned the brushed chrome handle and pushed the door inside, then closed the door behind me. I waited for a couple of seconds to make sure I was indeed alone, then moved further inside and turned on the light.

Both beds were made. There were no signs of luggage or personal belongings. I fed my hand between the thick fabric of the curtains and held it open far enough to make out a few figures on the street by the waterfront. Where earlier I'd seen the flashing light, now I saw the outline of two men, one holding the other at gunpoint. Even from a distance I could tell the man with his hands in the air was Jack Jordan.

NINE

The scene was far worse than I'd expected. I needed to call someone—maybe the front desk, maybe 911—and tell them a man was about to be shot by the waterfront, when both men turned and faced the hotel. The man with the gun was Louis.

As I stood there, as still as I could, I realized that I'd made the biggest mistake of my life by turning on the lights. If they'd been able to signal to each other earlier, then surely they'd be able to see me, now.

Jack Jordan clasped his hands together and brought them down on the back of the other man's head. Louis fell to the ground and dropped the gun. Jack picked it up and jogged up the hill.

I knew I couldn't go back to my room. That would be the first place Jack would look for me. I started to leave, tripping over the corner of the bedspread. I heard a sound by the door, mechanisms inside the keycard lock that had tumbled. I was trapped.

I scanned the room for a hiding place. If I got past the beds and found the opening between the curtains I could open the sliding door to the balcony and hide outside, but for how long? The idea of falling down four stories was about as appealing as being caught in the room red-handed.

My right hand was on the closet door, which slid open an inch. As the door to the room opened up, I squeezed into the closet and slid the door shut behind me. I waited, with my heart pounding in my chest, for someone to open the doors and expose me.

I pressed myself backward, despite the pressure of something already in the closet digging into my thigh. A safe, probably, or luggage stand. I knew the importance of remaining still despite the discomfort. I only wished the occupants of room 419 had taken the time to hang up their clothes so I'd have something to hide behind.

"I'm telling you, the light came from this room. I've been watching the windows all night. I didn't make a mistake," said a male voice.

I froze. It was Jack.

"I don't know what kind of game you're playing, but there's nobody here," said another voice. It was the other man from the elevators that first day. That meant Louis was most likely the person who'd been knocked out by the waterfront.

"Check the balcony," commanded Jack. "I'll check the closet."

I felt the hand connect with the door to the closet before it slid to the side, leaving me face to face with Jack Jordan.

His eyes went wide for a second. He held a finger up to his mouth to silence me, then mouthed the words. "Trust me." He slid the door shut as quickly as he'd opened it, leaving me speechless.

"You're wasting my time, Jordan. Where is she? I've traveled a long way and spent a lot of money and I'm not leaving without her."

"I'm telling you, something's not right. We have to get out of this hotel."

"No. This time I'm telling you what we're going to do. You're going to give me the lady and I'm going to walk out of here and head back to Los Angeles. She's going to be on a plane by midnight and I'm going to be a millionaire."

"That's not what we agreed on."

"Yeah? Well, things changed when you knocked out Louis. He's been keeping an eye on the lady since she got here and now he's out of the picture thanks to you. Makes me wonder if you've been planning a double cross all along."

"Louis is the one who pulled the double cross. I was just taking care of myself," said Jack.

"Not sure I believe you."

There was silence, and I pictured the two men facing off, each with a pistol aimed at each other, waiting to see who was going to shoot first.

"Get the lady," commanded the unnamed man.

"First I want to see the money," said Jack.

"The money's in the safe in the closet. You'll get it when I see her."

Before I could figure out how exactly I was going to master the art of transmogrifying, there was a knock on the door. I held my breath and listened for something, anything.

"See who that is," said Jack.

Soft footsteps, muffled in carpet, walked past me to the door.

"It's the cops," said the other man.

Another set of footsteps crossed the room, then, a dull thud. Someone grunted, then something large fell to the floor.

I couldn't see how any of that was good.

The closet door slid open. Jack Jordan grabbed my wrist and pulled me out. Grey suit's body lay slumped on the floor.

"There's a man in a uniform outside this door. He is not a cop. He is not going to expect to see you. Use that element of surprise and get out of here. Go to your room—no." His eyes darted to my face and past me to the door. "Go to the lobby. There's a diner across the street. It won't be empty. Go there, get a booth, and wait for me. Don't talk to anybody, don't tell anybody what's happened."

"You're crazy!" I hissed. I pulled away from him, but his grip on my wrists tightened.

"There's no time for me to explain what's going on. You have to trust me."

"No," I said in a barely audible whisper. "The cops are here to help me."

The pounding on the door resumed. Jack stepped away from me and peered through the peephole, then came back. He put his hands on my forearms and squared me off. "When you open the door, look at the officer. Decide for yourself if you should trust him or not."

"Why should I listen to you?" I asked.

Unexpectedly, he put his arms around me and hugged me, pinning my arms to my sides. "I know I'm asking a lot of a stranger," he whispered in my left ear. He released his hug and stepped back, waiting to see what I would do next. "If you believe he's a real cop, then tell him everything." He let go of me.

I stepped away from Jack, my back pressed against the wall. I searched his face for something reassuring but saw nothing. I stepped past him. When I reached the door, I looked to Jack one last time. He wasn't there. I tucked my chin and braced myself. I pulled the door open.

I recognized the uniformed officer who stood in the hallway. He had longish blond hair tucked behind his ears and a mole under his left eye. He was the man who had driven me from the airport to the hotel. He was not a cop.

Jack was telling the truth.

I sucked in a deep breath of air and pushed past him as instructed, then ran as fast as I could into the hallway, down the hall, to the elevator. My knee pulsed, but adrenaline kept me moving. I jabbed the up and down buttons by the elevator. The up button lit up first and I hopped inside and pressed Door Close. My heart pounded in my chest like a chef pounding out a chicken breast with a wooden mallet. I didn't care I was going up without an escape route. Up was better than where I had been, and after going up my only problem would be getting back down. I could deal with problems like that.

And then elevator stopped on the eleventh floor. The doors eased open and a fresh new problem confronted me.

I was face to face with Brad.

TEN

I slapped at the panel of buttons on the wall. One of the buttons screamed the alarm. The doors slid shut. Brad didn't move. I gulped deep breaths and punched the lobby button repeatedly, as if it would make the elevator travel faster. I looked around the elevator for a hidden security camera, something that indicated that there was a chance I wasn't really all alone. Aside from the reflection of the brunette stranger in a cowboy hat and Dodgers t-shirt in the mirrored ceiling, I saw nothing.

When I landed in the lobby several older couples stood around in nylon jog suits and bright white sneakers, as if their trip to Carmel had required new workout clothes. A police officer stood by the front door. I didn't know if he was real or not. My knee throbbed but I headed past the early birds to the front door anyway, in search of the crutches I'd abandoned in the front garden beds earlier that morning.

"I don't know who she is," I heard. I looked in the direction of the voice and saw Kitty from the front desk talking to a man in a black suit and tie. "She was here right before Louis left. He found her crutches out front. I don't know where she went."

"Did you see her leave the hotel?" asked the man.

"No."

"Can you describe her?" he asked.

"She looks like, well, she looks like that," She pointed to a poster from *Midnight Lace* that hung on the wall of the hotel. By her feet a small dog wound circles around her leg, circling her with a blue leash.

"She looks like Doris Day?"

"Pretty much. She has fluffy blond hair and a cute freckled nose. She's thin and wore a floral dress. She smiled a lot."

The man studied the poster on the wall for a few more seconds. "Always liked her," he said, as if he were talking to himself.

I stood to the side of the column, weighing my options. On one hand I could approach the man talking to Kitty, tell him what I'd been through, and hope he was somehow able to help me. There had to be a reason he was asking her about me. On the other hand, I didn't know *why* he was asking about me. I caught my reflection in the glass frame of the *Midnight Lace* movie poster and gasped. Brown streaks from the temporary coffee-hair color ran down the side of my face like skinny sideburns and dripped onto the collar of the t-shirt. I looked a wreck.

And suddenly I knew Brad hadn't recognized me.

I inhaled deeply and blew the air out of my mouth. I straightened my posture and walked out of the hotel as though I was balancing a book on the top of my head: confident, smooth, injury-free. The doctors had told me I would know when I was well enough to start walking without the crutches, and right now, I knew. Even though pain shot through my leg at evenly spaced intervals, I faked good health until I reached the sidewalk, then crossed the street and entered the diner Jack had mentioned.

A rotund man in a stained apron approached my table. I ordered a cup of coffee and a Denver omelet before realizing I had no money to pay. I unzipped the small red and white cotton purse I'd slung across my body, hoping Elli had left behind enough emergency cash to buy me breakfast in a somewhat overpriced diner in Carmel By-The-Sea. I didn't come up with any cash, but I came up with a small black velvet pouch.

With my right hand shaking, I felt the bulging contents through the velvet. As if the shaking was contagious, my left hand shook as I undid the knot in the drawstring. I fed two fingers into the small opening and spread the fabric apart, then looked inside at the base of a small light bulb.

Not what I'd expected.

The waiter returned and filled the chipped beige coffee mug on the table with steaming hot coffee. I dropped the pouch into my lap and covered it with my napkin. I couldn't tell if he'd seen it or not, but until I knew what it meant I didn't want anybody else to know I had it. I leaned in and busied myself with pulling the top off a small plastic cup of creamer, then dumped it into my mug and stirred. I kept up the routine until the waiter was back behind the counter, then tapped the spoon on the side of the mug and set it into onto the table.

What did it mean? I wondered. Had this pouch been filled with a diamond at one point like Jack had told me? And if so, where was it now? Had it ever been in the pouch? Or had this been a double-cross all along?

I drank from the chipped coffee mug and considered other questions. Where had the pouch come from? Even if I didn't agree with her choice of baseball teams, it seemed unlikely that Elli, the very stranger whose luggage I'd ended up with, was really a jewel thief and a double-crossing smuggler. But how else could I have come to be in possession of this pouch?

I closed my eyes for a second and thought back over what had happened earlier. I'd hidden in the room, in the closet. Jack had been the one who exposed me hiding in the closet. He asked me to trust him and he arranged a way for me to get out of there. And then he hugged me.

He must have planted the pouch on me during the hug.

I'd been oblivious to everything at that moment—everything except getting away.

It clicked into place. He was the one who'd told me to stay in my room. He was the one who knew my story, who pretended to protect me by asking the operator to screen my calls. It had been his idea for me to disguise myself, so no one else would recognize me. If he'd hidden the pouch on me, nobody else would think I was connected to him when he came to collect.

And one last thought hit me. It had been his idea for me to go to the diner.

A collection of bells announced new customers entering the diner. I looked up at the door and clutched the black velvet pouch tightly in my left hand. Jack headed directly toward my table, followed by the man in the black suit from the lobby.

ELEVEN

They slid into the booth across from me. I felt like a scared rabbit must feel when hunting dogs close in. A small, vulnerable animal with no avenue for escape.

"You did good back there," said Jack.

"Who are you people?"

"We have to leave, Ms. Night," said the man in the suit.

"I'm not leaving with either one of you until I know who you are and what this is about."

The two men looked at each other, then the man in the suit nodded at Jack.

"Madison, I want you to meet my partner," Jack said. "This is Special Agent Hamilton Reed."

"Ms. Night, you are in possession of something illegal. You need to come with us."

"The only thing I'm in possession of is a light bulb. You want it? It's yours." I fished my fingers into the black velvet pouch, then set the small bulb on the table next to the salt shaker.

"Keep your voice down, Madison," Jack said.

The two men looked at each other. Jack stifled a smile. Agent Reed stood up. I looked back and forth between their faces. Agent Reed sat back down. Jack put his forearms on the table and leaned in.

"What are you afraid of, Mr. Jordan?" I asked in as casual of a voice that I could muster. I used his last name on purpose. I didn't want to feel like we were on comfortable terms anymore. I wanted to go back to the strained formality we'd had yesterday. I reached out and palmed the light bulb and put it back into the pouch. "Surely you don't think I had anything to do with—with—with the disappearance of the lady," I finished.

Agent Reed's eyes widened. "The lady?"

"Yes. The lady who came from Dallas. Mr. Jordan knows who I mean. Don't you?"

Jack turned to the special agent. "Get us some coffee. I need to talk to her alone."

Agent Reed slid from the booth and took up a position at the counter. He briefly spoke to the cook, then raised a knee and half-sat on a worn green vinyl swivel stool with rust peeking from the joints. They weren't half bad, those stools. Sand the rust, redip them in chrome, reupholster the vinyl—

"Give me the pouch."

"Sure," I said. "I can't see why anybody would want it anyway."

I set the pouch on the table in front of his arms. He kept his arms crossed for a few seconds while he considered it. "When did you realize it was a light bulb?"

"When I looked inside. I wanted to know what this is about," I demanded. I expected him to refuse or to clam up.

"Why?" he asked, catching me off guard.

"Why what?" I repeated.

"Why do you care? It has nothing to do with you."

"You lied to me. When I told you about Brad Turlington, you said he was a figment of my imagination. That's not
true. When I ran past the cop outside of 419, I came face to
face with him. It's him. I know it's him. *I know it's him.*"

Jack leaned forward. "Describe this guy to me."

I closed my eyes for a second, breathing in the memory
of Brad. "Tall, thin. Curly black hair. Sideburns. Glasses. He
has on an orange plaid shirt and khaki trousers. Purple con-
verse sneakers. He's wearing a gold watch, a vintage Rolex
and he smells like Old Spice. He must have gotten caught in
the sun yesterday because the tip of his nose is sunburned." I
was surprised by the level of detail I recalled of Brad from the
split second I'd seen him in front of the elevator.

"What did he do when he saw you?" he asked.

I opened my eyes and stared at the chipped coffee mug.
"Nothing. He didn't recognize me," I said quietly.

Tears filled my eyes, tears I tried to blink back. Instead,
they overflowed and ran in streaks down my cheeks, dripping
bronzer-colored drops onto the white napkin in my lap. I
swiped at the tears and inhaled sharply through my nose.

"Wait here." Jack slid from the booth and joined Agent
Reed. I willed myself to get control of my emotions.

I hadn't wanted to believe it was over, but after I'd left
the hospital, I wanted nothing more than to move on. In time
I'd stop looking for him around every corner. With time I'd
learn to shut myself off so this would never happen again. I
had come to Carmel to get away, to make a break, to clear my
mind. I'd been emotionally vulnerable when I'd landed at the
airport and I'd let that vulnerability turn into a paranoid roller
coaster ride. Enough. I would not let Brad continue to erode
my emotional stability.

I looked out the window of the diner toward the hotel. Men in painter's caps and overalls carried supplies through the front door. A white van was parallel-parked in front of the lawn. On the side of the van was a familiar logo: Pierot's Interior Design.

I knew the logo. I knew it all too well. Pierot's was the furniture store where Brad and I had met back in Philadelphia, when it was owned by Mr. Pierot, soon to retire. It was where Brad had taken me under his wing and taught me about Mid-Century Modern design, the store that I ran while he traveled the country taking interior design jobs. It was where I learned how to acquire merchandise for resale without breaking the bank. I narrowed my eyes as I wondered what the van was doing in California, then remembered when he'd ordered the signs—magnets, really—with the Pierot's logo, to add a bit of professionalism to his freelance team when he took jobs around the country.

Jobs around the country. Like Carmel By-The-Sea.

To Doris Day's hotel, currently under renovation before the annual Carmel Art Festival. That's why it had all seemed familiar. Brad had bid on this job when we were still together.

Another man opened the van and put a floor lamp inside. I recognized the style immediately, a product of the fifties atomic era that captured the whimsical impact that technology and outer space had inflicted on interior design. It was my single favorite design aesthetic, the one category where Brad and I disagreed when he trained me to be an interior decorator. He liked the minimalism of the mid-fifties, the planes of Danish modern, the simplicity of George Nelson and Charles Eames. I did too, but I was also drawn to the sillier aspect of midcentury design: yellow walls, sputnik lamps, radial clocks, donut phones, and boomerang tables. Where Brad's sense of decorating was rooted in wood, mine was rooted in laminate. He'd tried to change my tastes but it didn't work. Eventually, he blamed it on my fascination with Doris Day movies, something he knew he could never undo.

And here I was, sitting in a diner across the street from the hotel Doris Day owned in Carmel, watching a man in overalls carry furniture out of the hotel, furniture that by anybody's account had been handpicked to make the place something special.

In a moment, as I sat watching the man in overalls load items from the hotel into the back of the van, it occurred to me that everything I'd seen, everything I'd heard, everything I'd imagined, made sense if I trusted one man's information.

"Jack," I called out suddenly. "I know where to find the diamond."

The two men looked at me. I stared out the window, glued to the scene. I was right. I knew I was right. Now I just needed to make sure the right men believed me.

Special Agent Reed paid for my coffee and we left.

"Follow me," I said, heading back to the hotel.

As I walked, I scanned the crowds of people already pouring onto the streets. Carmel By-The-Sea was a walking town, and by the looks of it, it was a morning town, too. Cars were in the way more than they were a convenience factor. I'd noticed most of the tourists parked their cars when they arrived and didn't move them again until the day they left.

A bicycle cop poised on his bike in the driveway between two hotels. His uniform matched that of the officer who had come to the hotel room earlier.

"Excuse me!" I called out to him before Jack or Agent Reed could respond.

The officer shielded his eyes and looked at me, but didn't respond. I crossed the street and closed the distance between us until I was right in front of him.

I took two deep breaths, one for courage and one because I was out of breath, then started talking. "Hi. I'm Madison Night. I'm staying at that hotel and there's something criminal going on in there. Some kind of jewel heist. Did you see the men who followed me out of the diner?" I asked.

I turned to look behind me and shielded my own eyes. Jack and Special Agent Reed were gone. I turned back to the officer, who was still staring at me. "I don't know where they went. Anyway, this is important. See that van in front of the hotel?" I pointed to the Pierot van. "Those aren't real decorators. They're faking it. They're pretending so they can take something valuable from the hotel."

The officer looked over my shoulder, then back at me. "I'll keep an eye on them."

"So you believe me? Do you want to take my name down for a statement or something?"

"That won't be necessary. I'll take it from here."

That's exactly what I wanted to hear. "Thank you officer," I said, all the while knowing the man I spoke to was faking his own identity as much as I had been faking my information.

I returned to the hotel lobby and found Jack and Agent Reed sitting by the fireplace. I wasn't terribly surprised they'd left me. I eased myself into the seat in front of them. My back was to the concierge desk.

"Here's what's going to happen—" I started.

"Ms. Night, with all due respect, you're not the one calling the shots," said Special Agent Reed.

I crossed my arms and leaned forward. "Do you know what's going on?" I asked Agent Reed. When he didn't answer, I turned to Jack. "Do you?" I waited a couple of seconds.

"Listen to the lady, Reed," said Jack.

Agent Reed crossed his own arms to mirror my body language. I wasn't sure if he was going to say something or not. He didn't.

"The cop I approached out front is not a cop but he thinks that I think he is. I told him to follow the men unloading the furniture from the hotel because they're not really decorators and they're trying to smuggle something valuable from the hotel."

"Why do you think those men aren't really decorators?" Reed asked.

"They are decorators—that's the point. The fake cop doesn't know that, so now he's off on a wild goose chase."

Neither Reed nor Jack reacted, so I knew the information I'd spoken so far wasn't news. I continued. "The diamond isn't in that van. It's safe. But if you want to make sure the men from 419 don't get her, we have to act fast."

"Ms. Night, thank you for your help, we'll take it from here," said Special Agent Reed. He stood up from the table and turned to Jack. "I'm going after the decorators."

Jack nodded, then turned to me. "What else have you figured out?"

Jack Jordan had been the only person to investigate what I'd said so far. If anybody was going to listen to me, I suspected it would be him.

"The men loading the truck out front are probably free-lancers. I didn't think about that when I made the reservation, but Brad's been applying for jobs around the country, trying to build his client base and his reputation. The hotel is under renovation. Brad must have hired freelancers when he took the job. He doesn't have a staff in California and it would be cheaper to hire someone here then to pay people to travel with him. You already told me Brad's not on the guest list. He's here to work, not to play. That's why his name isn't in the system. He's not part of the problem."

"Go on."

"The cop on the bicycle was wearing the same uniform as the man you knocked out upstairs. It says Carmel, NY."

"And you told him to follow the decorators?"

"I figured it was the only way to get him away from the hotel."

"But they're decorators," Jack said.

"Yes. They're probably putting items in temporary storage so they can paint the place."

He held out a hand. I grabbed it and he pulled me up. "Were you telling the truth, Ms. Night? You know where the rock is?"

"Yes."

"Good. I'm going to visit our friends. You get the rock. Meet me as soon as you can."

"You want me to get it?"

"You're the one who's undercover," he said, with a hint of a smile pulling at the corner of this mouth.

"Where do you want me to meet you?"

"I'll let you figure that out, too."

He left before I could tell him I seriously had no idea.

TWELVE

Jack Jordan walked past the front desk while I remained in the hotel lobby. Kitty glanced up at him but didn't seem to recognize him. It was a piece of the puzzle now falling into place. Kitty belonged behind that desk as much as I might have. She was part of the problem, not part of my solution. Jack must have known that all along.

I caught my reflection in the glass of a poster hanging on the wall. Undercover was an understatement. I pulled the cowboy hat off, only to expose matted hair that lacked its usual fluffy volume. Instead of running my fingers through it like instinct told me to do, I set the hat back on my head and tipped it forward to shield my eyes.

I walked past the front desk to the elevators, stopping for a second by marble table in the hallway. I picked up the squat ugly lamp and pulled the brown rubber electrical cord from the outlet. I wound the cord around my left wrist and pressed the call button, silently urging the elevator to get me out of there before anybody noticed what I'd done.

The elevator seemed to take an unbelievably long time to finally arrive, though it couldn't have been more than a minute.

The doors slid open and I got inside and jabbed the door close button repeatedly. I did not want company on this ride.

Just as the doors were about to slide closed, a hand fed between them, triggering the sensors. NO! The doors slowly retracted and my worst fear came true.

Brad stood in front of me.

I fumbled with the buttons on the control panel with my free hand as though I were searching for the one that would open the doors, all the while staring down, refusing to make eye contact. I accidentally hit the alarm button, sending a caustic ring through the shaft of the elevator well. The elevator didn't move. Brad stared at the lamp in my hands.

"Is that from the hotel?" he asked.

I looked at the lamp and nodded, the cowboy hat shielding most of my face.

"Most people take a bathrobe." He leaned into the elevator and pushed the alarm button, cancelling the siren. He looked at the squat ugly lamp again. "Southwest design…I guess some people like it."

There were so many things I hadn't said to Brad at the top of that ski slope. I stared at the object, for fear if I looked at him I would say something I'd regret. Then Jack Jordan, my savior Jack Jordan, appeared like an angel in the hallway. He stepped into the elevator between me and Brad

"Take the next elevator, man," he said.

"Excuse me?"

"The lady and I want to be alone."

"Sorry, man," said Brad, backing away from us into the lobby. The doors shut, leaving him on the outside and me on the inside with Jack.

"Was that your guy?"

"Yes."

He nodded once, then punched the 4 on the panel. "What's with the lamp?"

"What do you think is with the lamp?" I replied.

His face lit up as though it had been plugged into the now empty socket in the hallway.

I spent the last day of my vacation in the Carmel By-The-Sea Police Department surrounded by official looking men in black suits, white shirts, and skinny neckties. The only person in the room I recognized was Jack. He'd lied when he said he was head of security for the hotel. In reality, he was an FBI agent on the tail of a ring of jewel thieves.

The men and women behind the jewel smuggling had been working Carmel for months. It was a touristy town, a good place for outsiders to congregate, because everybody was an outsider, literally. They blended in by not blending in. The two men I encountered by the elevator the very first day were the men who anticipated going home with a fourteen carat diamond from the Barbary Coast.

I answered a lot of questions, and asked a few, too. I didn't get satisfactory answers. What I pieced together was the cops—the fake ones—had been planning a bait and switch all along. They knew the diamond was coming in to Carmel and the switch was happening at the hotel. Kitty worked for them, keeping lookout from the front desk. Her role allowed her access to the switchboard, to see what calls were going where. When Jack requested that no calls go through to my room, Kitty connected the dots. They didn't know how I figured into their overall plan, but my presence—and my reliance on the head of security—told them I was a part of it all. Once Kitty tipped them off, it wasn't difficult for them to keep tabs on me.

I asked if Louis and Grey Suit were the buyers, but they didn't tell me. I asked if the fake cops had been arrested and they didn't tell me that, either. I asked who had put the diamond in the lamp, when Jack had put the velvet pouch in my handbag, and if anybody knew how close they'd come to letting a team of decorators walk out of the building with a fourteen carat diamond. I'd worked out a plausible explanation but it was obvious nobody was going to validate my theory.

"Ms. Night, tell us why you refused to cooperate at first," said Jack.

"Mr. Jordan, with all due respect, nothing I've been told over the past four days made any kind of sense to me. I couldn't trust anybody."

"So what changed?"

"It wasn't one thing, it was a bunch of things. Those men kept showing up and asking about me. And then you kept showing up and telling me they weren't asking about me, which I wanted to believe, but couldn't. And then the phone calls started, and you told the receptionist to hold calls to my room, but when I called her back, she claimed she hadn't seen you since you returned from your vacation. You have to admit, from my perspective, things were very confusing."

"When did it click?"

"When I was at the diner, looking out the window at the hotel. I saw the van for the decorators and I realized why Brad was here. As soon as I realized you were telling the truth about him not being a guest at the hotel, I thought about everything else you'd told me. And once I determined everything you told me could be strung together as the truth, I realized everything else I'd been told had been a lie. From everybody. So I knew I could trust you and nobody else. Not the cops. Not the operator. Not the men from the elevator."

"That's a big mental leap to make."

"It was more than that. Once I started looking around, I saw things that didn't make sense. One of the cops had long hair. I don't think police officers are allowed to wear their hair long. Their uniforms were wrong. I'd overheard Kitty talking to one of them, and realized she hadn't addressed him like she would a police officer, so she must have been involved."

"Not much gets past you, does it?" he said. I detected a complimentary tone but I couldn't be sure.

"What do you mean?"

"Most people don't see that much of the world when they're on vacation."

"It's a compulsion. It's what I do."

"How's that?"

"I'm a decorator. I look at a room and I see what fits and what doesn't. I take away the problem and I'm left with the beginning of a solution."

"Is that how you figured out about the lamp?"

"I've hated that lamp since I first arrived. I saw it while waiting for the elevator after checking in. It's so out of place with the rest of the hotel. It didn't work, either. And once I realized the thing in the black pouch was a light bulb, I knew where to find the diamond. The lamp by the elevator was the perfect spot. Who looks at a lamp in a hotel? Nobody."

"You did."

"I already told you what I do." I stared at him for a couple of seconds, wondering if he expected me to continue or if he would keep pointing out that my brain didn't work like other people's brains.

"It didn't make sense the decorators would leave the lamp. Especially Brad. He hates southwest design. This would have been the first thing he replaced. Someone must have told him to leave it."

Jack checked some notes he'd made on a white lined tablet. Creases on his forehead deepened as he flipped back a couple of sheets, holding a black and gold ballpoint pen in one hand, touching different places on the paper as he scanned the contents. Four sheets back he tapped the paper a couple of times, looked at me, then looked back at the paper.

"You know this Brad guy pretty well, don't you?"

"I thought I did. Why?"

"I can't share anything from his statement with you."

"Meaning what? Did he say something about me? Did he recognize me?" I asked, leaning forward.

Jack didn't speak. Instead, his silence fell onto my questions. The longer they hung in the air, the more I regretted asking them.

"Never mind. I don't want to know—"I started.

Jack reached out and placed his hand on top of mine. "He said coming to this hotel was the second biggest mistake he'd made in his life."

I looked down at my hands, resting in my lap. "Did you look inside the lamp? Did you find it?"

"We did."

"And?"

"I can't tell you any more than that."

I understood.

I finished up with the men in the room and signed a piece of paper agreeing not to talk about what had happened during my vacation. When I was finished, I followed a uniformed officer out front where an attractive man with a light brown ponytail stood by the street. He wore a long sleeved navy and white striped shirt and faded blue jeans that were stained with dirt at the knees. Next to him was a small, green, energy-efficient car.

"Are you Madison Night?"

"I am."

"I'm Merritt. Jack asked me to give you a ride back to the hotel."

I looked behind me to the police station where Jack Jordan stood framed out by the white brick archway that surrounded the front door. The keystone over his head looked like a crown. He smiled, nodded, and waved.

"Can you wait here for a second?" I asked Merritt. I walked back to the police station. Jack met me half way.

"Ms. Night, you're a heck of a woman. Forget about Turlington. I bet you'll find someone way better for you."

"What about you, Mr. Jordan? I seem to remember you had somebody who wouldn't appreciate you spending the night in my hotel room."

"Yeah, I do." He put his hand on my upper arm and gently turned me to face the ponytailed man. "That's him."

And suddenly, the last of the mystery surrounding my vacation in Carmel was solved.

THIRTEEN

When it came to Ms. Elliott Lisbon's suitcase, I was at a loss. Most of her belongings had been dirtied or destroyed. Everything, in fact, with the exception of the Dodgers t-shirt. I'd asked the hotel to launder the t-shirt for me. I wasn't sure how to explain the rest of the clothes, and, finally, I figured out a way to not explain them at all.

Dear Elliott,

I am not in the habit of opening stranger's luggage or using their personal belongings as my own, so it's with more than a little embarrassment I admit to having done just that. I can't explain why I did so, only that I had to, and I'm well aware of how thin that sounds. I'd tell you about the FBI and the investigation, but they told me I can't, so I'll say the only thing I can. I'm sorry. I wish I could return your items in the condition they were in when I first opened your suitcase, but that's no longer an option. Since almost everything you had packed still had tags on it, I'm hoping it can be replaced. I'm also hoping this will cover it.

Sincerely,
Madison Night

I clipped ten one hundred dollar bills to the side of the paper and tri-folded it, then unfolded it and included another thousand dollars. I had no idea how much Eliot's items had cost her and since I lived in vintage sixties ensembles and dresses scored at flea markets and estate sales, I wasn't the go-to person for quoting the price of a new western ensemble. There had been a reward for my help in the capture of the jewel smugglers, and even though I wouldn't see the money right away, by now I trusted Jack Jordan enough to know it would arrive. Two thousand dollars would probably replace the contents of my entire closet if I didn't count my collection of hats, but somehow, when I considered the violation of Elliott Lisbon's personal belongings, two thousand dollars didn't seem like so much.

I printed the stranger's name in neat architectural drawing-like letters across the front of a crisp ivory envelope I'd bought at the local stationery store. I gently folded the t-shirt and set it in the middle of the suitcase. Before putting the letter into the suitcase I added a postscript:

PS: It might be fun to meet face to face sometime, but in the interest of full disclosure, you should know I'm a Phillies fan.

I sealed the envelope and set it on top of the t-shirt, then closed the suitcase.

PART 2:
SWITCH BACK

An Elliott Lisbon Mystery Novella (prequel to *Board Stiff*)

by Kendel Lynn

ONE

The wheels of our flight touched down in Waco, Texas at half-past eleven on a very late hot August night. I would've been so much happier had those wheels touched down at Dallas/Fort Worth since that's where we were heading, but after circling most of north Texas for over two hours to avoid a batch of wicked storms, I was happy enough to just get on the ground.

It took another thirty minutes for an airport employee to push the stairs out to the jet and another twenty to herd us into the small terminal. My traveling companion, Mrs. Zibby Archibald, who at eighty-six still looked ducky in her best pink suit and matching hat, sat next to me on the worn pleather bench while we pondered our options.

"Well, that wasn't so bad, dear," Zibby said. She pulled a tissue from her oversized pocketbook, then snapped it shut on her sleeve. "Though I'd think a flight from South Carolina would be shorter."

I patted her leg and tried to eavesdrop on the group of pilots in the corner. The place was jammed with cranky, crumpled passengers, none of whom planned on visiting Waco in the middle of the night. Including the pilots of no less than seven jets who'd been diverted over the course of the last six hours to an airport without the personnel to handle any of it. They'd closed at nine that evening and had no plans to bring the crew back until morning.

"Air traffic control isn't even responding to my calls anymore," one pilot said to another.

"Yeah, same with the base office and the union. I radioed a friend diverted to Abilene. Says DFW's shut down until dawn, no matter what they told us earlier. Book the first hotel you can get because they're going to be scarce."

Two little boys in the seats across from ours fought over a sticky handheld video game. Their mother snifled and sneezed out a half-hearted warning, which they ignored.

I inched closer to Zibby and lathered on my nineteenth layer of hand-sani in the last four hours. Even though being in the airport made my skin itch, I reminded myself it was one level better on the germ-scale than being on that airplane.

A lone security guard walked past me to the pack of pilots near the gate. He raised his hands and spoke to the crowd. "Ladies and gentleman, due to the weather, flights won't resume until first thing tomorrow morning. Please keep your boarding pass to re-board your flight. The airport will be closing in twenty minutes. After you leave the secure area, you may not return until we reopen at five a.m. Thank you."

He said all this with the practiced air of a flight attendant instructing passengers to fasten their seatbelt by placing the metal flap into the buckle via posted placard. Clearly this wasn't the first group of flights to land at Waco's gate in the middle of a storm.

After telling the crowd everything it did not want to hear (no, there are no nearby hotels; no, you may not sleep inside the terminal; no, there are no restaurants open this time of night; no, the luggage will not be retrieved as there is no way retrieve it; no, I do not have a manager you can speak with), he calmly walked through the angry throng toward the security gate.

"So glad the rain stopped," Zibby said. "It would be terrible to get my new hat wet after all this. I bought it just for the Honeysuckle Festival."

"Agreed," I replied, but I was much more worried about Zibby than I was her honeysuckle hat. She couldn't sleep on the hard dirty sidewalk in the dark, surrounded by strangers and whatever else slinked through the night. How could they just dump us without our bags, then shoo us into the night like unwanted refugees?

My brain tried working out different departure scenarios as I gathered up my one belonging, a small quilted handbag, and helped Zibby to her feet. We limped our way to the exit with only minimal pushing and shoving. By now most of the crowd was too tired and hungry to put up much of a fight.

Once we hit the fresh air outside, I eyeballed the last two spots on a metal bench at the far end of the sidewalk. I was about to make a dash for them when a woman with big brown hair and a big bouncy bosom approached us.

"Miss Zibby," she hollered, then wrapped her in an exuberant hug.

"Why, Rita Whitaker," Zibby replied. "What a pleasant wheel of fortune running into you. Our flight was diverted and that pilot plunked us right where you are."

"It's why I'm here, sugar," Rita said. "Gonna take you both into town. I couldn't leave y'all stranded way out here."

I was so relieved, I wanted to hug her myself. "I'm with Zibby, definitely our good fortune to see you. And you must be from Little Oak?"

"You bet. Lived there my whole life. Own the inn where you're staying, assuming you're Miss Elliott Lisbon with the Ballantyne Foundation. I was almost to DFW to pick y'all up when the storms ripped through the sky like a hurricane in July, so I kept driving. Figured it was either going to be Waco or Abilene, and I'm tickled as a turnip it wasn't Houston."

She tucked her arm in Zibby's and looked around our feet. "Y'all have any bags?"

"Oh yes," Zibby said. "I brought three suitcases for clothes and one for shoes, but they won't let them off the plane. Guess we'll just have to follow the wind."

"We really appreciate the ride," I said as we walked through the small lot to a very large pickup truck. "I wasn't sure what we'd do for the night. Any idea what they'll do with our luggage?"

"Sure, happens all the time. They'll fly it over in the morning. I'm driving down to DFW first thing to pick up more guests. I'll grab it then."

We clamored into the enormous cab, after I gave Zibby's behind a nice big shove, and pulled out onto the dark highway, about a hundred fifty miles from our destination.

"Oh Rita, I'm so excited to be back," Zibby said. She belted herself in with her pocketbook on her lap. Inside the seatbelt. "I've missed my dear Bea. How's her spirit?"

"Not the same since Austin passed," Rita said. "But she's doing her best. She's so looking forward to your visit. We all are, ready to show off the town."

"Elli, wait until you see Little Oak. So beautiful. And vibrant! It's the envy of all Dallas."

"Only take about three hours to get us there," Rita said. "Might want to take a doze if you can."

She didn't have to tell me twice. I tilted my head against the passenger window as the black asphalt sped by. I closed my eyes and hoped my travel theory held solid. Sometimes when a trip starts out terrible, you get the bad out of the way and the rest is all rainbows and cupcakes.

Turns out for this trip, there would be no rainbow after the storm. Just more storm.

TWO

We bumped into Little Oak, Texas just before three a.m. My legs were cramped, my eyes were scratchy, and my left hand was tingly from Zibby sitting on it. We unloaded Zibby at the Carter ranch first, which took all of three minutes since she had no bags or carry-on, then rode about a mile down the road to the Little Oak Inn.

It wasn't until I entered the living room lobby that I realized the inn was more bed and breakfast than hotel.

Rita went behind the counter and rifled for a pen. "You must be exhausted, sugar." She fiddled with some paperwork, which I promptly signed and exchanged for a key.

"This is the best room I've got," Rita said. "Top floor, spectacular view. And we'll have fresh frittatas and biscuits in the morning." She peered over the counter, then looked back at me. "Right, no luggage. Have your claim ticket? I'll drop it off in the morning."

I blinked back at her trying to remember where my tag was, then slowly dug it out of my hipster handbag.

"You're all set then. Have a good sleep and don't forget to come down for breakfast. I'm serving my homemade honeysuckle jam with fresh sweet butter."

My mouth watered as she pointed to the center staircase and I trudged up to the third floor with key in hand. It took three tries to wiggle that sucker into submission, but the door finally creaked open and I creaked inside.

Without a toothbrush or hairbrush or clean tee to sleep in, I simply set my handbag on the nightstand, stripped off my skirt, flipped off my flip flops, and fell onto the lumpiest mattress this side of the last century.

Seventeen things bumped in the night and I finally opened my eyes to the bright glaring sun sooner than I wanted. A room full of windows, and not one had a blind or a curtain. Not even a single sheer to prevent the room from turning into an oversized sauna. I rolled over and and cursed for a solid minute the fate that brought me to the surface of the sun in the middle of summer.

As of a month ago, the Ballantyne Foundation on Sea Pine Island, South Carolina was the proud owner of Little Oak, Texas. As Director of said Foundation, I volunteered to trek to the town, attend the Cattle Baron's Ball, and thank Bea Carter and her family for their generous donation.

And generous it was. We'd never received an entire town before. I'm not sure any charitable organization had. And I certainly didn't know what to do with it. Zibby Archibald, one of our most cherished benefactors, joined me on the trip as it was her late family friend, Austin Carter, who had bequeathed the town upon his death. Not sure how the rest his family felt about it, but I'd soon find out.

I dragged myself out of the lumpy bed and into the tiny bathroom. And by tiny, I mean tiny. The door was about half-size of normal and hit the back of the sink when it opened. After I availed myself of the facilities, I realized I had nothing else to do. No clothes, no toiletries, nothing to unpack and nothing to change into. The tee I slept in was rumpled and stained with the airline's finest red wine. I didn't drink it fast enough before we hit the storms and managed to splash half a glass right down the front.

But my paisley skirt survived without a drop, and my flip flops would do just fine. I spied the sliver of bar soap I used to wash my hands and bit back another shiver. Based on the layer of dust that had coated the wrapper, I wasn't sure the last time the room was cleaned. Or with what. But soap is soap, right? Even if it tightened my skin like leather on a football, I'd still be clean.

I was debating my options when I heard a loud knock on the door.

"Hellooo, Elliott?" Rita of the homemade honeysuckle jam and fresh butter called through the door. "You in there?"

"Hi, Rita," I said, trying not to sound the like morning grump I am.

She handed me a small baggie with a miniature toothbrush and toothpaste and a small black comb. "Small delay with your luggage. Some kind of storm glitch, tags don't match or something. My girl needs a quick description, contents and all that, says it'll make it go faster."

I cringed at the thought of some strange girl rifling through my things, but then remembered I brought a one of a kind suitcase. "It's easy to spot. A bright turquoise hardback Samsonite, white trim, metal latches. Let her know it's the only one."

"Will do. See you in a jiff," she said and shut the door.

I locked it behind her and rushed my bounty straight to the bathroom.

After a seven minute shower in which the water alternated between a comfortable rapid boil and just shy of freezing, I hopped out and dried myself on a thin scratchy towel. The skin on my face was indeed so tight, I probably looked ten years younger than my quite youthful forty years.

It took longer for me to comb out my auburn snarls than it did the whole rest of my morning routine. But I slapped on yesterday's clothes, grabbed my handbag and went downstairs, determined to shake off my bad mood and all this travel drama. There were frittatas in my future.

The dining room bustled like an Original Pancake House on a Sunday morning. Folks filled every table, including a bar along the back wall. I grabbed a plate, but quickly realized most of the food was gone.

I snagged the last half a biscuit and waited in line for a glass of fresh squeezed orange juice.

Rita came over just as I drained the last drop. She wore a bright blue scarf over her tall brown hair.

"You gotta get down here earlier. The frittatas go fast. Lots to do today."

"This all for the Honeysuckle Festival?"

"Oh no. That was canceled in favor of the Broken Spoke Casino Rally." Rita bounced through the dining room and into the living room lobby and I trailed behind. "Wait 'til you see the plans the tribe drew up. Custom felt tables and authentic saloon chairs for the slots."

"An Indian casino, in Little Oak?"

She dug through several boxes of party supplies at the counter. Poster boards, markers, balloons, and a spool of red ribbon nearly a foot wide. "Yes, ma'am. Going to be bigger than the one in Oklahoma. We'll even have a real sports book in the gaming center."

News to me. Especially since the Foundation now owned the town and we had no plans to build any kind of gaming center. We actually didn't have any plans at all.

I was about to mention that when she gave a questioning head tilt toward my tee. "No extra top shoved in your purse then, huh?"

I liked to travel light and not lug fifty pounds of personal belongings through travel worn public places. But as I followed her gaze to my filthy shirt, I thought perhaps a larger over-the-shoulder bag wouldn't kill me.

"I'm hoping there's a boutique nearby, somewhere I can buy a new shirt, maybe some toiletries?"

The main door opened and two men with a large banner balanced between them struggled through. I rushed over to hold the door open while they wrestled the banner across the threshold.

"Sorry it took so long, Miss Rita, but we got it here before the Honeysuckle opens," one of the men said. "Usually get these things turned around in a couple weeks, but we've been swamped."

"No worries at all. Y'all did just fine," Rita said as she signed the delivery slip.

Two women came in and grabbed the boxes of decorations while a teenaged girl in short shorts started cleaning the desk.

Rita talked to me over her shoulder. "Most of the stores closed, sugar. Town's nearly shut down. Might be able to find something next door at the gift shop. Think Gilda's got some adorable t-shirts. You need anything, anything at all, you just ask. Tell her I sent you," she hollered as she scurried through the back door.

The sky was bluer than the Caribbean Sea and just as tranquil. The temperature had to be close to ninety-five and it wasn't quite ten a.m. On the bright side, the humidity was low. A nice break from the thick air back in South Carolina. Several trees lined this end of the town square. Interestingly, they were all crepe myrtles with not a single oak among them.

The town square was more of a town rectangle. The Little Oak Inn sat center between Little Oak Gifts and Little Oak Grill. Two rows of shops flanked each side of a long brick lane. Rita wasn't exaggerating. Nearly every shop was empty. Their windows dusty from abandonment, small closed signs tilting sideways on the doors. I thought perhaps a tumbleweed might blow by except for the activity far down the road. Trucks and vans parked all along the curbs and men unloaded equipment, or perhaps pipes or building materials.

When Zibby told me about this unique donation to the Ballantyne Foundation, I didn't quite know what to think. She spoke of a town square bustling with shops and restaurants. With summer festivals and a thriving tourist trade. If anything, the profits would go straight to the Foundation where we would direct them into one of our many causes. She never mentioned a casino replacing the bustling boutiques. Perhaps a lease already in place?

After two minutes in the sun, I popped into the gift shop for supplies and possibly a little scoop. With Rita busy, I needed someone to tell me what was going on.

The bell tinkled as I walked in and a short round lady walked out of a backroom. Her frizzy blond hair probably hadn't seen its natural color since she graduated high school sometime when Eisenhower was president.

"How you doing this delightful day?" she asked.

"Well, I'm having a t-shirt emergency and I hear you're the one to the rescue."

She glanced at the enormous red splotch that covered most of my upper half. "Sure, sugar, got a nice selection in our souvenir section." She pointed me to an array brightly colored almost all cotton shirts.

I mostly hid my blanch as I carefully picked through the round rack.

"You here for the Revival or the Rally?" she asked.

"I'm actually here for the Cattle Baron's Ball. Came in last night."

She sighed somewhat wistfully. "The Ball used to be the event of the season. Hard to believe this will be our last one. We've got so many things changing around Little Oak these days."

"And I'm another change, but a good one. I'm Elliott Lisbon with the Ballantyne Foundation. We inherited your town."

"Well, howdy-do. I was hoping to meet you today. We worried your flight might get turned around with the storms and you wouldn't make it. I'm Gilda Hays." She stretched out her hand to shake mine, enveloping it in both of hers, all soft and warm and germy.

I smiled on the outside, but inside I couldn't wait to rip into my mini hipster and lather on a good coat of hand-sani.

Discreetly, of course.

"Nice to meet you, Gilda." I stopped shirt shopping and lowered my voice one degree. "I had no idea most of the shops were out of business."

"Oh sure. Everything's being replaced, either with the Light of the Rock megachurch or the Broken Spoke Casino. Don't know which project will get the green light. Though my money's on the church, no pun intended. No chance the state's going to allow gambling, no matter who ole Chief Fannin knows. But don't go telling Rita that. She's on the casino side of town."

"When did all this—"

The tinkle of the entry bell interrupted me and my final words of "take place" faded into Rita's high-pitched burst.

"Elliott," Rita cried. "You've got to get to the ranch. Zibby called up, said the Sheriff himself is arresting Bea right as I speak. For murder. Arresting her for Austin's murder like she's a common criminal and not the town matron hosting the largest party this side of Dallas." She remained in the doorway, arms splayed across the opening, one hand gripping the door, the other the frame. "Can you believe it?"

I could not believe it. Considering Bea's husband, Austin Carter, died of a heart attack over a month ago. I grabbed the tee my hand rested on and shoved it at Gilda. "I'll take this one."

She pulled it off the hanger in one swift move. "You can change right through there, and don't worry about paying. We'll settle up later."

I ducked behind a curtain into a makeshift dressing room and threw on the tee. A red crewneck with bold blue letters spelling out "I Love Texas" with a ginormous heart around the word love.

Rita offered to toss my stained shirt back into my room as we rushed up the sidewalk. "I've been best friends with Kathy Lee, that's Bea's daughter, since we were toddlers crawling around the big oak tree. Bea's like a second mother to me. Please tell them I'll be by as soon as I get someone to cover the inn."

She started back inside when I grabbed her arm. "Can you call me a taxi?"

"Oh mercy me, we don't have taxi service. Used to have the trolley, but not since two seasons ago. I lent the truck out this morning, but you can take my scooter." She dug the keys from her pocket and handed them to me. "It's round the side there."

"Thanks, Rita. And where am I going?"

"Straight up Oak Street, round the oak tree, can't miss it."

I jogged over to the far side of the gift shop and indeed, there was a vintage Vespa with chipped turquoise paint and a yellow helmet. As soon as I fastened the chin strap, I zipped down the brick road at a perky twenty-five miles an hour. The sun baked my skin so quickly, it was like riding through the Sahara on an electric camel.

The rows of desolate shops ended about a quarter mile into my ride, replaced by wide stretches of land with small subdivisions tucked behind a tree line on both sides of the road. Tall big top tents were going up in front of each set of trees. An army of workers hammered stakes and hoisted poles as if the circus had come to town, while another group set up tables down the center of the road.

I weaved around the obstacle course of party planners, and a minute later saw the lone oak tree. It had to be taller than a three-story department store and nearly as wide. The tree sat in the middle of a well-tended garden bursting with fragrant summer roses and leafy purple kale.

A wide iron gate fronted a drive on the other side, the words Broken Spoke in an arch above the entrance. I followed the winding drive a quarter mile and spotted Zibby sitting on a bench near the front door of a traditional white plantation house. Magnolias and crepe myrtles shaded an expansive lawn surrounded by black ranch fencing. Three white utility vans took up most of the circle drive which hummed with an army of caterers and crew in uniform.

I nestled the Vespa on the walkway, half on the lawn, half off. "Zibby, who's arresting whom?"

"Oh, Elliott," she said. She gripped her handbag tight in one hand and a silk handkerchief in the other. "The police are dragging Miss Bea away. I didn't know what to do but call you."

"Rita said something about a murder."

"Austin's! They think she killed her own husband."

The door flew open and a little blond woman waved us in. "Is this your gal, Zibs, the one who fixes things?"

"Oh yes. This is Elli Lisbon with the Ballantyne. She really knows her trouble."

"Well, then, get on in here. Kathy Lee's pitchin' such a fit, Sheriff's about to cuff her up next to Mama Bea."

THREE

The little blonde walked back through the open door, clipping along the marble floors in a pair of shoes so high, I thought she might tip over. And yet she still only reached my elbow.

"I'm Jolene Carter," she called over her shoulder. "You're just in time to stop the nonsense."

I followed her down the hall and into a bright sunroom just off the kitchen.

"They think Mama Bea killed Big Daddy. Now that's nothing but a bunch a ballyhoo, isn't it, Sheriff?"

A man in a tan uniform, presumably the sheriff, tipped his Smokey the Bear hat and set down his coffee cup. He rose from his seat at an elegant side table and gestured to an older woman sitting at the same table, wearing her Sunday best, sipping from her own pretty porcelain cup.

She smiled at me. "You must be Elliott. I'm Bea Carter. Zibby simply adores you, so of course I'm sure I will, too. She says you're just what we need to untangle this pickle I'm in. Can I getcha cup of coffee or a scone?"

I eyeballed a platter of raspberry white chocolate scones and blueberry muffins surrounded by dainty dishes of butter, clotted cream, homemade jams, and fresh honey. I instantly forgot about all those frittatas I missed out on earlier. Who needs eggs when there are chocolate scones?

"Sheriff, I think we should get on our way," Bea said. "Traffic's going to be sticky if we wait much longer."

"Okay, then. Already called Austin Jr.," the sheriff said. "He'll meet us at the station, have you out before sundown." He tipped his hat and escorted Bea from the room, her arm wrapped in his as if they were taking a stroll through town.

Zibby and I took their empty seats at the table and I poured us coffee. I don't usually drink it, as I prefer my caffeine cold, but I didn't want to make a fuss.

A tall woman with a jet black bob marched into the room, her voice as powerful as her steps. "If you think I'll just stand by and let you drag my mama out the back door like a presidential assassin on election day, you got another thing coming Sheriff—" She stopped mid-rant and spun toward Jolene. "Where the hell did he go? Did you let him haul her off to jail, Jolene? I'll give that Sheriff the what for if he took Mama without waiting for me."

"Oh relax, Kathy Lee," Jolene said. "A.J. will have her out this afternoon. Now the good Lord's watching and I'm sure He doesn't appreciate you threatening the law."

"Well, you can tell the good Lord I don't appreciate this cataclysm on the day of Big Daddy's Cattle Baron's Ball."

"You can tell the Lord yourself," Jolene said.

The two women stood toe to toe; Jolene in sassy red stilettos and Kathy Lee in sturdy black pumps. And as with me, the top of Jolene's big blond hairdo-ed head reached Kathy Lee's elbow at best. The two women looked about the same age, I'd guess close to mine for the both of them.

"You just set yourself to prayin' and all kinds of good will rain down on you," Jolene said. "Once we open the Worship Center, you can join the beginner's bible group with the eighth graders. Start you out slow so you don't get confused."

"I know my bible as well as you," Kathy Lee said. "And there will be no Worship Center. My daddy fully supported me building the Broken Spoke Casino on this land and I will not stand by and watch your money grabbing 'preacher' ruin this town." Kathy Lee said preacher with a full body swing and exaggerated air quotes.

"You've got a lot of 'not standing by's' flying around this room for someone who appears to be standing still as stick in dry mud while our mama gets thrown in the pokey."

"She's my mama, not yours. You married my brother, not my family. And dry mud is plain old dirt."

I decided to wedge myself into the argument before the fine china started to fly. "I'm confused," I said to no one in particular. "I thought Zibby said Austin died from a heart problem."

"He sure did," Jolene said. "Pair of oversized scissors right to the heart. That's murder, even in Texas."

"Always knew his heart would give him trouble," Zibby said. "Most generous man I ever knew." She refilled her coffee cup, then added a small spoonful of butter and stirred.

"So very generous," I said. "We, me and the Ballantyne Foundation, are extremely grateful for the donation. Though, maybe it's me, but I don't remember anything in the documents about a church or a casino."

Kathy Lee arched an artfully plucked brow at me. "If you think I'll stand by—"

"Oh good heavens, Kathy Lee," Jolene said.

"—and let you steal away my inheritance, then you've no idea who you're talking to."

"I kind of don't, actually," I said. "Though I'm assuming you're Bea and Austin's daughter?"

"Their *only* daughter," Kathy Lee snapped.

"I'm just like a daughter, you ask Mama Bea," Jolene said. "Met A.J. at Sunday School near twenty years back and we've been inseparable ever since."

"My brother, Austin Jr., is an attorney and he's drawing up a suit against your 'foundation' right today," Kathy Lee said with her hands still mid-air. "You won't be able to steal my town."

"I'm not stealing anything from anybody," I said with a more defensive tone than I intended. "The Ballantyne Foundation is quite reputable, I promise you." So just calm down with the air quotes, I mentally added.

"That may be," Jolene said. "A.J. and I fully support all kinds of charities. But I'll tell you, it's mighty un-Christian like for you to fly in here and steal away our family's legacy."

"Again, not stealing," I said. "It was donated. Honest. There are legal documents involved. Besides, it's still in probate, so no need to sue me."

"Big Daddy's barely gone a month, his heart torn in two, and he'd roll right over if he knew this was happening," Jolene said. "And poor Mama Bea. Hurtin' all over again."

"Oh, this can't be happening," Zibby said. "Miss Bea will miss the party tonight. Her own celebration of Austin. It's an unfair supervention."

"Damn that Bobby Wainwright," Kathy Lee spat out, her face so red I thought her head might pop off. "This is all his fault. Jealous as a schoolyard bully and twice as mean."

"Who's Bobby Wainwright?" I asked.

"County prosecutor," Jolene said. "Been at odds with the Carter family ever since he and A.J. played opposing quarterbacks for rival Tots football teams. Silly really, but there you have it."

"It's not silly, Jolene," Kathy Lee said. "Purposely trumping up charges to ruin the Baron's Ball is spiteful and malicious."

"Well, he's also the only one in the county not invited, so that probably didn't sit well," Jolene said.

"I forbid that man to step foot in this house or these grounds," Kathy Lee said.

Jolene leaned forward as if telling me a secret, girlfriend to girlfriend. "Kathy Lee's never forgiven him for not asking her to prom senior year. Took her rival instead."

"Oh shut up," Kathy Lee said. "This isn't about the prom, it's about the Cattle Baron's Ball. And Mama missing it the first time in her life, unless your outlandish plan somehow works."

Zibby dabbed her forehead with her silky kerchief and Jolene looked at me with her head tilted to one side.

"Outlandish plan?" I glanced from Zibby to Kathy Lee, then back to Jolene. I casually brushed at my face in case I had something stuck on my cheek.

They continued to stare at me expectantly.

"Well, don't just sit there, Elliott, wearing that tacky tee like you're about to clean out the barn," Kathy Lee said.

"Don't just sit here, what?" And even though I knew I looked ridiculous in my thick cotton Texas tee, I thought it rude of her to point it out. "My luggage was delayed, thank you very much."

"I sure hope you're not wearing that to the Cattle Baron tonight," Kathy Lee said. "The dress code requires more class."

"I certainly know how to dress for an event." I tried to keep the huff out of my voice, but I don't think I succeeded. I wanted to mention some of the Ballantyne parties we were hosting just this year like The Gatsby and The Palm & Fig Ball, but I feared they'd assume I was offering up invitations.

They still stared, so I asked again, "What plan? What am I missing here?"

"These two think you're going to prove Mama Bea didn't murder Big Daddy," Kathy Lee said.

I turned to Jolene. "So you're not suing me?"

"Of course we are," she said. "But first things first, sugar."

FOUR

"I'm not sure what I can do for you," I said, though I finally understood what Jolene meant earlier when she said I was the one who "fixes things."

"I'm not, either, but you can start by giving us back our town," Kathy Lee said. "Then we won't have to make a judge force it from you."

"Don't let Elli fool you, girls," Zibby said. She added another spoonful of butter to her coffee and spread honey on a scone. "She performs disconnected inquisitions for all us board members."

"Discreet inquiries," I corrected.

"She's a crackerjack for the Ballantyne," Zibby continued. "Helps find all kinds of missing things. Someone pilfered my dear friend's Pomeranian right from the beauty parlor in the middle of the day. Only took Elli two weeks to get her back. Isn't that right, dear?"

"Well, then naturally, let's choose the doggie detective to save my mama," Kathy Lee said.

"She also got Jeremy Turco out of the slammer twice and helped catch the island's only band of kleptomaniacs. But that's all blither blather. The Pomeranian kidnapping was personal and our Elli put her heart into finding that adorable Biscuit."

"I also have a Bachelor's in Criminal Justice and am working toward my PI license in South Carolina. Clocked nearly four hundred hours." I didn't mention I needed over six thousand to meet the minimum requirement and I didn't know why I was trying to impress them.

"We've got to do something," Jolene said. "Not like we have any private investigators in Little Oak. Barely any folks left in a twenty mile radius. And Mama Bea's due at the revival for the Worship Center on Saturday."

"You mean the Broken Spoke Casino," Kathy Lee said. "I'm already suing the Ballantyne, I've got no trouble suing you, too."

"Good Lord in heaven," Jolene said. "A.J. isn't going to sue himself."

"He's not the only lawyer in Texas," Kathy Lee said.

"This will never do," Zibby said. "Your daddy would be caddywomped seeing you two fight, and now poor Bea will be hung in the town square for murder."

"It's the electric chair," Kathy Lee said. "We don't hang people anymore."

"It's lethal injection," Jolene corrected. "Has been since before we started high school. You'd know that if you went to church more."

"Ladies, please," I said. "No one is hanging in the town square. But you people sure do know a lot about the death penalty. Especially if you talk about it in church."

"An eye for an eye, sugar," Jolene said.

I was beginning to think I'd need something stronger than butter in my coffee to get through this day. "I could use the experience, I guess," I said doubtfully. Not sure the Texas law enforcement folks would appreciate it, but probably couldn't hurt to ask questions, put in a little effort. Might at least stop them from suing me and the Ballantyne.

"Why did the sheriff arrest Bea?" I asked. "Did he tell you what evidence the prosecution has against her?"

"Oh sure," Jolene said. "Sheriff shared it over coffee first thing this morning. They've got Mama Bea's fingerprints all over those deadly scissors. Hers and only hers. Not surprising since she still had a firm grip on them. Was leaning over Big Daddy when they found him."

Well then. Not much room speculation. "Why would she want to kill Austin?" I asked.

"She wouldn't," Jolene said. "Loved that man since he took her to their first dance in grade school."

I was sensing a theme. Seemed everyone in this family met their spouse over the swings in the playground. Perhaps options might be limited in such a small town.

"Do either of you know anything else about Austin's death?" I asked.

"Whole town knows," Jolene said. "Can't paint your toes without everyone chiming in about the color."

"Big Daddy was in his private office at the back of the house, late on a Friday night," Kathy Lee said. "Mrs. Alden was asleep in her room when she heard Mama scream."

Jolene plopped into a chair at the table and helped herself to the last scone. "Mrs. Alden's been taking care of the Carter family since the Civil War or thereabouts." She leaned back and crossed her legs. "Everyone in Little Oak thinks it's the will. That Mama Bea killed him for the inheritance."

"But the Ballantyne inherited," I said. "Was it a secret?"

"It was an accident," Kathy Lee said. "Big Daddy just overreacted. Wanted us to stop fighting over the town. It's our legacy, Little Oak. We were supposed to agree on its future, but when we couldn't, he tried to scare us by putting this silly Ballantyne clause in."

"Why did he choose the Ballantyne?" I asked.

"My favorite charity," Zibby said. "Austin knew how I love the Ballantyne and wanted a solid recommendation."

"No better charity than the Light of the Rock," Jolene said. "Don't know why he didn't settle this himself."

"Because it's better to give back to the people who originally owned the land, the Big Spring Choctaw."

"If that's your argument, then you know full well God owned the land first," Jolene said.

"And He gave it to the Choctaws," Kathy Lee said.

I asked Zibby to walk me to the door while those two squawked like a couple of crows on a wire.

"Elli, dear, thank you so much," Zibby said. "I know Bea couldn't have done something so shuddersome. It broke my heart to see her dragged off like that."

"No worries. I'm sure we'll work this out."

I definitely needed to do something. Mr. Ballantyne would be caddywomped himself to have his reputation besmirched by accusations of stealing an entire town. And even though Zibby wasn't related to the Carter clan, she was related to Edward Ballantyne. And if she wanted help, then I was on the case.

And fast. I had a return ticket on Sunday morning and no amount of Texas charm would keep me from boarding that plane.

FIVE

I didn't have a lot of time and even less to go on. If Bea wasn't going to inherit, and she had loved Austin since toddlerhood, then why would she kill him? Must be a reason. And if she was holding the deadly scissors while the body was still warm, and the county had enough to arrest her, then I was pretty sure she did it. Aside from every hillbilly stereotype on cable tv, most law folks know what they're doing. Sure, that sheriff looked sheepish, but also quite serious. And probably not the type to tolerate a meddling islander on a scooter.

But since he was driving Bea downtown, plus booking and all the accoutrements that followed, I probably had a good four hours to poke around. Take him all day before he'd even hear about me, and really, who would tell?

I pulled out my cell and dialed Tod Hayes, Ballantyne Administrator. He picked up on the third ring. He didn't even say hello.

"How is it you're there not one full day and trouble's already found you? Not sure that's what Mr. Ballantyne had in mind when he sent you as the welcome wagon."

"I'm not a welcome wagon."

"Clearly," he said.

I could picture him in his tidy office beneath the stairs at the Ballantyne manse, sitting ramrod straight in a crisp white shirt in a room right out of the Addams Family.

"But wait, what trouble are you talking about?" I asked.

"The lawsuit, of course. Unless you're in more than one kind of trouble."

How did he hear about the lawsuit already? They hadn't even drawn up the papers. "Who told you about that? I just found out not ten minutes ago."

"Reporter out of Dallas called for a comment. Said there's a rumor 'out-of-state carpetbaggers were swooping in like buzzards over roadkill.' I believe you are the buzzard in that scenario."

"You are shitting me," I said. I snatched the scooter helmet off the back with one hand while I balanced the phone with the other.

"I shit you not," Tod said. "Mentioned Tate Keating's name, says they're working together."

Tate Keating handled the social scene for the Islander Post on Sea Pine Island. And by social scene, I meant mostly Ballantyne events and how to make them sound scandalous.

"Better clean this up before nightfall," Tod said. "I kept it from Mr. Ballantyne while he's out shooing turtles back into the sea, but you know someone will track him down."

"I'm on it. Can you do me a favor? Find out—"

"No more favors. I've got three words for you: Mitzi's Baby Shower."

Right. I'd actually forgotten that tiny favor. When one of the most-cherished and wealthy Ballantyne patrons asks you to host her highly anticipated baby shower, you smile and say you'd love to. But once I booked my flight to Dallas, Tod then inherited the not so enviable task of hosting the shower—for Mitzi the Labradoodle and fifteen of her best canine friends. Once Tod reminded me of that tidbit, I was kind of surprised he even took my call.

"Well, yes, there's that," I said, "but you refused to go to Texas."

"They kill people in Texas."

After the casual conversation about the death penalty this morning, I couldn't argue with that one. "If you could find out anything on Austin Carter's death, I'd be forever in your debt. His murder created this salmagundi. From the Ballantyne inheriting the town to the Ballantyne stealing it."

"I believe that's your specialty, and you better get cracking. Tate said he had something spectacular lined up for Sunday's edition. And you're already forever in my debt. I have little faith you'll live long enough to pay it off."

"Oh calm down and help me already," I said, but I was talking to myself.

I scrolled through the contact list on my phone and called the Islander Post. Tate didn't answer his extension, so I left him an urgent message to call me back. Then I strapped on my helmet and puttered down the drive. After being Director of the Ballantyne for over seven years, you'd think I'd be better prepared for reporters who can sniff out a scandal faster than a beagle searching for bacon.

Speaking of bacon, I got back into town right before lunch on Friday afternoon. And though I'd just had a platter of fresh baked scones, I decided to drop into the restaurant first. The best place to find locals who like to gossip. Plus, I'm not one to turn down an opportunity to eat a meal.

I tucked the scooter back in its spot as Rita poked her head out the front door of the Little Oak Inn. "Just put your suitcase up in your room. Took my girl a while to find it, but she finally plucked it out of the international bin. You do know they make them with wheels now?"

I thanked her and debated running up for a clothes swap, but the restaurant was only one door down. I was already out front and a hot mess, so I decided to wait until I got cleaned up for the Ball later that afternoon.

The interior décor of the Little Oak Grill matched the outside. All western and Texas and wood. A long bar made natural wood spanned the entire back wall with tree stumps for barstools. A dozen matching tables were scattered across the main floor which was covered in crushed peanut shells.

I ponied up to the bar, grateful to be in the air conditioned room, even if surrounded by more longhorns than at a UT football game.

"Howdy, little lady," an older gent in a well-worn Stetson said. "Getcha some tea?"

"Pepsi would be better."

He opened an old-fashioned Coke bottle and set it in front of me. "This here is Coke country. Hope it'll do."

Of course it is. I nodded and smiled and tried to look charming even though my hair stuck to my forehead in a most unattractive manner. And I'm pretty sure I had a small pool of sweat on my upper lip. "Kind of quiet around Coke country. Where did all the shopkeeps go?"

"Town's in a bit of flux. But we've still got the best burger in the state."

"I'll take it. Medium rare with cheddar and a splash of barbeque sauce if you've got it."

"My sauce is homemade," Gilda said as she slid onto the stool next to mine. "It's taken first place at the State Fair three years running."

"Your sauce?" I asked, while the old cowboy went in back, presumably to cook up my lunch.

"Yep. The Grill's been in my family some sixty years now. I bought the gift shop on the other side of the inn when the owner retired, oh, I'd say fifteen years ago, I guess. I run the gift shop most mornings and spend my afternoon's over here." She patted her plump thighs and laughed. "Should probably consider putting more salads on the menu, but this here is Texas, and I do love my barbeque."

"I met the Carter sisters this morning," I said and took a deep swig of my Coke. "Seems they aren't all that happy about the Ballantyne inheriting the town.

"Those girls have been squabbling like territorial hens, pecking each other until their feathers fly off. And it's gotten even uglier since poor Austin passed away. Sin versus redemption. Half the town wants the sin, the other half the redemption."

"And no one minded giving up their businesses?" I asked. "Seems like that might create animosity toward Austin." And give nearly every Little Oak resident a motive to kill him. Those left, anyway.

"Austin was a gentleman and a businessman," Gilda said. "Offered most of us a nice deal. Bought out the leases and a guaranteed job at the new venture." She leaned forward, even though we were alone at the bar. "A hundred thousand dollars. And if they wanted to move, he'd buy their house. Can't beat that."

"Not in this economy," I said.

Gilda went into the kitchen and emerged with my lunch platter: a juicy burger and a mound of skinny fries. It took all my willpower to eat slowly.

"Folks took those deals before Austin could even sign the contracts," she said.

"That's a whole lot of money going around," I said. "But still. Might be tough to be forced to give up your life's dream to work in a church. Or deal cards at a casino. Certainly someone wasn't happy."

"Well, sure. Miss Rita didn't quite like it," Gilda said. "Thought they were missing a big opportunity to keep her landmark hotel, which fits with either the church or casino."

Seems Gilda herself might fall into that same landmark category, since her gift shop and restaurant were part of the same landmark building as the hotel. Her businesses also fit with either a church or a casino. I noticed Gilda said Austin offered "most" a great deal and if "they" wanted to move.

"Gilda, you mentioned something about a revival?"

"Oh sure, Reverend Kincaid's holding a tent revival tomorrow to get folks excited for the Light of the Rock. Everyone's coming out for it and the ribbon cutting's supposed to be this weekend. Unless they're headed to Chief Fannin's Broken Spoke Casino Rally. I guess just as many folks happy to cut that ribbon as well."

Gilda grabbed a Coke for herself. "But enough about the town, what happened with Bea?"

I started to fill her in on all things Bea and the Sheriff, when Zibby came through the door, breathless as if she ran all the way from the ranch.

"Oh, Elliott! You have to go down to the Town Hall," she said. "It's all gone to hell in a picnic basket!"

SIX

I took one last longing bite of my burger and followed Gilda and Zibby out the door. They hurried through town, oblivious to the dry heat baking the street like a gigantic pizza oven.

I, on the other hand, was not oblivious. The poly fifty-fifty tee I wore neither breathed nor wicked away. But it did do a nice job of insulating my body heat. On the bright side, I probably lost a solid five pounds on the way to the Town Hall.

We walked into a very packed square room set up with about a hundred metal folding chairs. Nearly every seat was filled, and it seemed as if each person had something to say. All at the same time. A stage at the front of the room held a wood podium where two men stood, one on each side.

Easy to figure out who they were. The Reverend Kincaid, a tall white man with a perfect tan and movie star teeth, wore a beautifully tailored suit, a bright sash across his shoulders, and held an oversized white bible in his hand. Chief Fannin, an equally tall man but with dark skin and jet black hair in two long braids, wore jeans and a plaid shirt with a suede vest with feathers dangling from the fringe.

Gilda went straight to Jolene at the front of the room, gave her a big hug and took a seat on the right side of the room, the Reverend's side. I noticed my hotel host, Rita, next to Kathy Lee, front row on the other side. I slid into a seat in the back with Zibby.

The Reverend pounded the podium with an oversized gavel. "Folks, let's simmer down. No sense getting worked up when we need to get this worked out. The Light of the Rock teaches toleration with those who need our guidance to lead them away from sin. Shall we pray?"

"I mean no disrespect, Reverend Kincaid, but the Big Spring Choctaw tribe does not promote sin," the Chief said. "We offer a way to bring a new life to our people, and to yours."

"No way the Lord or the state will allow it," Jolene said, standing to address the room. "Those God-fearing folk shut down Speaking Rock lickety-split, and they stand with us in this battle. Y'all are wasting breath doing the devil's work."

Kathy Lee jumped to her feet. "Stop preaching as if the good Lord is only on the right side of the room, for Pete's sake. We've got the votes to pass the casino bill, and we'll be next in line to open after Speaking Rock. So sit down and let us get on with it."

"Yeah, sit down, Jolene," a woman in the crowd shouted. "You're not the only God-fearing woman in this town. Stop acting like it."

"You watch your mouth, supporting that sin wagon hitching its way into town," another voice called out.

That didn't even make sense. I leaned over to speak to Zibby. "Why are they arguing when the Ballantyne owns Little Oak now?"

The man in front of me stood so fast, his chair pushed back and cracked into my knee. "Hold on. What do you mean someone else owns this town?"

"Who? Town's been in the Carter family since they pulled up in a stagecoach. Someone swooping in now Austin's dead and gone?"

"Indeed," another voice added. "City folk with their fancy private jets and money bags, I bet."

Private jet? I remembered circling Waco for two hours just last night, and based on the meal for purchase option, I'm pretty sure I was flying commercial.

"We did not steal anything," I said, stepping into the aisle. I smoothed my Texas tee and tried to look friendlier. "We're not city folk. We're a reputable charity on Sea Pine Island, South Carolina. We help children, the underprivileged. We're spiritual people. I'm a spiritual person. Austin Carter generously donated this lovely town to us in his will."

"We'll see about that, red-headed woman," the Chief said. "We do not take kindly to strangers stealing land that does not belong to them. Our history has taught us to fight harder for what is ours. This land belongs to the Choctaw."

"You want to build a casino, not a reservation," someone piped up on the church side of the room. "And Big Spring isn't even a real tribe. We're building a church and you can't stop us."

"Like hell," someone from the tribe side said.

"Friends, you're forgetting about the Ballantyne," Gilda said. "Seems they may not want either one."

"I don't think Edward Ballantyne gambles much," Zibby said. Her hands gripped her purse strap so tight, I feared her knuckles might snap right off.

"We've got that covered," the Chief said. "Filing an injunction first thing Monday."

"A joint injunction," Kathy Lee added. "Followed by a lawsuit against the Ballantyne for fraud. Throwing in collusion and coercion as well."

"About time somebody did something," the man in front of me said. "My store's been closed nearly three months, I'm ready to move on already. Can't sit around all day every day counting weeds, now can I?"

I put my head in my hands and tried to breathe slowly. This was not what I envisioned for my quick trip to Texas. And certainly not what Mr. Ballantyne expected. More lawsuits and jail time being bandied about than a Law and Order episode.

"Something illegal going on? Maybe this town needs a watchdog," a man said as he walked down the aisle, toward the podium. He looked casual, but nicely tailored, in slacks and a sport coat. And cowboy boots instead of dress shoes.

"Bobby Wainwright, how dare you show your face," Kathy Lee said. "You get the hell out of here."

"Language, Kathy Lee," Jolene said in a stern but syrupy drawl. "The Lord's listening."

"And He isn't afraid of the word 'hell,'" Kathy Lee snapped back.

Jolene ignored her. "Good to see you, Bobby. Been awhile."

He tipped his gray cowboy hat. "Jolene, always a pleasure."

I started rubbing my temples to ease the tension that arrived with one Bobby Wainwright, county prosecutor and Carter nemesis.

"You can't be here," Kathy Lee said with such intensity, I thought she might actually stomp her foot. "This is private."

"Sign out front says meeting's open to the public," Bobby said.

"It sure as shit doesn't mean you," Kathy Lee said.

Chief Fannin moved closer to Kathy Lee in the front row to form a united front. "I must agree with Miss Carter, prosecutor. This is a town meeting and you are not a resident."

"Neither are you, Timothy Fannin," Bobby said. "Not sure how you weaseled into Miss Carter's good graces, but makes me wonder."

"My graces are none of your business," Kathy Lee said.

"They used to be," Bobby said. "Some habits are hard to break, like watching out for you. I may think your brother hasn't got a lick of sense when it comes to most things, no offense, Jolene, but I agree with him on this casino idea."

"None taken," Jolene said. She smiled a real charmer and sidled closer to the middle of the aisle. "You boys fighting doesn't bother me one bit. And it's encouraging to hear you taking up our cause against these sin wagers."

"We are not waging sin, Miss Jolene," Chief Fannin said. "We bring jobs to your town, and help our own people, a solid boost to both economical structures. We've long been in this region and our survival is pivotal to this program, thanks to Jolene and Austin Jr."

"But not Austin Sr., right?" Bobby asked. "Word is he didn't take to you very well. Was doing a bit of research on your 'Big Spring Choctaw' band and the results weren't coming in favorable."

Now there's an interesting tidbit. I made a note to do my own research on the Chief. While the Reverend Kincaid had salesman written all over his fancy religious sash, I hadn't thought about a wolf in Chief's clothing.

"None of this concerns you, Bobby," Kathy Lee said, her face as red as her dress.

"With both your parents, um, gone, I guess, someone needs to keep an eye on the family," Bobby said.

"Well, it sure as hell won't be you," Kathy Lee said. "Now where's my mama and why are you here?"

"Getting booked about now, I imagine. I came down to see what else I could find out."

Kathy Lee looked as if she'd been slapped at the mention of him booking her mother for murder. "You mean what else you can make up."

He surveyed the crowd, slowly making eye contact with nearly everyone in the first two rows. "If anyone has information on what happened to Austin, or anything else funny, you call me anytime."

"What do you mean?" Gilda asked. "I thought you had all the evidence you needed to arrest Bea."

"I do have plenty, ma'am. But there's always more. You hear me talking about the underworkings of this casino, and you've got this church project. Now I hear about a charity. Seems something's going on in Little Oak."

"Stop digging up trouble where none exists," Rita said, putting her arm on Kathy Lee's for reassurance. "You've done enough to this family."

He stared at Kathy Lee and their eyes locked for what seemed like a full thirty seconds. "You know where to find me." He strolled back down the aisle casually, not a care in the world. He slowed slightly when he reached me standing near the back row. "I'll be waiting to see the lawsuit filed against you. Might be some action the law needs to take." He tipped his hat and walked out.

"Oh Elli, what will happen to the Ballantyne if Edward goes to jail?" Zibby said. She put her hand against her pale cheek, and looked faint. "I just can't stand it. First Bea, now Edward. Do you think I'll be next?"

I stepped back to my seat and hugged Zibby. "It'll be fine, Zibby. I promise. No one's going to jail. Bea will be out sometime today, you heard the sheriff this morning."

"You're right," she said. "Supposed to be out by the time the shrimp cocktail makes its rounds at the ball tonight."

"See, we'll celebrate with cocktails," I said. "And I'll take mine without the shrimp."

"Sweetie, this town's dry," a woman next to me said.

"Dry?"

"Yep. No alcohol sold or consumed."

"Heaven help me," I said just as my phone rang. I glanced at the caller ID: Mr. Ballantyne.

"Heaven indeed," the woman said.

"Just knock it off like you're the only folks getting in…" another woman said.

I quickly slipped outside and answered the call. "Mr. Ballantyne, sir. So good to hear from you."

"Howdy, Elliott! How's things down on the ranch?" He asked in a booming voice. "You getting a big Texas welcome? Folks in Texas do things big, I hear."

"Yes, sir. A mighty big Texas greeting."

"I'm hearing grumbles about trouble with Bea Carter. I'm worried over Zibby, you know she loves Bea like a sister.

I'm afraid she shouldn't have made the trip. You watching over her? Her heart isn't what it used to be."

"One slight tiny hiccup with Bea Carter. I've got Zibby, sir." I walked down the street at a pretty quick clip, hoping he couldn't hear the hollers from the hall.

"What I wanted to hear. You take good care of her. I'm leaving for Mumbai tomorrow. Want to make sure this is wrapped up tight before I go."

"Zibby's great. The town's great. It's all great."

"Keep up the good work, my dear Elliott!"

"Yes, sir," I said, but he was already gone.

I looked around the abandoned street. It felt like a western town right off a Hollywood set. Ranch fencing made from wooden posts fronted the sidewalks as if you might tie up your horse while you shopped. Each storefront unique, some with pitched roofs, some with mock saloon doors. I walked up the sidewalk and wondered what made the Carter clan ditch their lively town after all these years.

And why wasn't anyone worried about Bea Carter? Did she really kill her husband? She seemed nice enough, and evidence or not, I couldn't see any motive. She just didn't have a horse in this rodeo. Unless that was her plan. She knew about the Ballantyne clause. So she kills Austin so neither child got their way, basically washes her hands of the whole thing. Might be pretty darn clever.

SEVEN

I wandered down the road in the hostile heat to the inn, the cool air welcoming me into the living room lobby. It sparkled as if Mr. Clean himself spiffed and shined in case the governor might pop by. The boxes of supplies were long gone, the room neat as a model home. I walked up the three flights to my penthouse suite impressed at the beauty of this small hotel. Until I entered my room.

Still paltry and stuffy and dusty. The ceiling fan pushed the air slowly around the room and I dropped onto the bed to enjoy the peace, if only for a few minutes. But I still had the Carter conundrum on my brain.

It wasn't actually insurmountable evidence that Bea was attached to the murder weapon when the maid walked in. Isn't that generally how it would go? If you see someone lying bloody on the floor, especially a loved one, you're going to rush over, try to do something. She screamed for help, Mrs. Alden came running. What bothered me more was that Bea didn't have a strong reason to kill her husband. Certainly others in this tiny town had more motivation.

Even Rita, proprietor of this very inn. She wanted to keep her business, not tear it down to make room for a church or casino. But then, so would Gilda, her storefront neighbor. If I used that reasoning, I might as well throw in most of the townspeople. And in the end, what good did killing Austin do?

Killing Austin came down to the will, who got what and when. With an entire town at stake, it had to be the motive. That line of reasoning pretty much ruled out Jolene and Kathy Lee. They each wanted their own project, not one of the Ballantyne's. It had to be better for them to keep trying to persuade their Big Daddy, rather than either of them to kill him.

And Austin's death probably wasn't premeditated. Must be a hundred other ways to off a guy rather than to jam scissors straight into his heart.

Someone was not happy with Austin Carter.

I reached for my phone and spent the next hour and a half researching the Reverend Kincaid and Chief Fannin, using my recently acquired PI researching skills and the magic of Google. My phone had limited internet capabilities—I didn't bring my computer since it's the kind that sits on my floor, not on my lap—but it was enough to discover that the Light of the Rock had a snazzy website with live and recorded podcasts and webcasts from their small church south of Dallas. They also sold inspirational books, coffee mugs, t-shirts, and offered more than a dozen ways to donate money. All very legit, if not a smidge flashy.

On the other hand, not much turned up on the Big Spring Choctaw or their chief. Only a handful of vague articles referencing their recent gambling establishment efforts buried in the back pages, and a simple landing page for the Broken Spoke Casino.

I used shorthand as I jotted notes on the little paper pad from the nightstand. BSC, Big Spring Choctaw. BSC, Broken Spoke Casino. Coincidence?

My phone beeped as my battery faded away and I checked the time. The afternoon had slipped away.

Remembering the Cattle Baron's Ball, I leapt off the bed and spotted my suitcase in the corner. I'd never been so happy to see that beat-up beauty. I rarely used it since it was without wheels and expansion capabilities, but I'd lent my modern bag to a friend and grabbed this one from a stack of collectibles in my beachside cottage. I sighed with relief as I popped the metal latches. I needed a long hot shower with all my favorite products. And to wear my own clothes.

I could not have been more shocked when I lifted the lid than if it had been filled to the top with stacks of counterfeit bills.

I stared openmouthed at the garments layered inside the rectangular box. Every item was black. And thrown haphazardly together as if airport security dumped it on the floor, then scooped it up blindfolded and shoved the whole lot inside.

Clearly this was not my suitcase.

I gently lifted the clothing out. A small black top. A small black skirt. A small black pair of jeans. So dark and tiny. Like a goth girl in the third grade. Or a supermodel. I held the pants up to my frame. A very short supermodel. With gorgeous shoes. A dozen thoughts crowded my brain: Whose stuff is this? Who else uses a vintage hardcover suitcase? Where are my clothes?

Oh my God, my clothes! The Ball was in an hour. I glanced at my Texas tee and started to sweat. I ran to the bathroom mirror. My hair was as frizzy as the before shot in a shampoo commercial and I only had flip flops. I can't wear flip flops to a ball. I remembered my earlier statement to Kathy Lee about knowing how to dress for an event.

I went back to the suitcase to double-check my options. I dug all the way to the bottom. Nope. All small and tiny and black. And I realized whoever packed this didn't use organized Ziplocs or put their outfits in sets. Why not put them in sets? Who is this person? I started to repack when I noticed a beautiful bottle of Kentucky whiskey tucked near the bottom. It was very expensive and sealed up tight.

So she's not a third grader.

And it was probably the only bottle of booze within ten miles. I wondered if I could get arrested just for possessing it. Perfect. Sued and arrested. Mr. Ballantyne might never let me leave the state again.

I called the airline and promptly received a recording letting me know in a most pleasant mechanical voice that my hold time would be thirty-five to forty-five minutes. Who would hold that long? I slammed down the phone. Which on a cell phone meant I very firmly pressed the red end button.

I bit back the first twinge of panic. No need to get all crazy pants. This was not my first clothes related crisis. After two calls to the lobby and one to the gift shop, I finally got Gilda on the line and explained my suitcase switch.

"Sure, I can help. I've got something even better than the gift shop. I've got keys to the Twice Around boutique up the block. Plenty of dresses ready to attend a ball."

"Thank you, thank you. Meet you in an hour?"

"Better make it forty-five, I don't want to be late. See you at the door. It's the second to last shop on the right."

I thanked her again and quickly washed my skirt in the small sink. I'd need it for tomorrow. I glanced at my wine-soaked tee from the airplane ride over and decided it needed more advanced attention than I could give it using miniature bar soap. I Heart Texas would have to do. After a quick wash and hang dry, I squinted at the flimsy soapy sliver.

I only hesitated about two blinks before I went straight to the fashionista's suitcase and fished out her liquids: soaps, lotions, and hair products. At the last second, I snagged the whiskey bottle and set it on the table. Just to look, not open.

Even though the water still alternated between hot and cold, it felt divine to scrub away the past two days using foamy soaps and slick conditioners. Once I was dolled up, I realized my clothes were wet from my sink hand-washing. Which meant I had nothing to wear to the dress shop.

I threw on the wrinkled wine tee and fashioned a skirt from a black scarf from the Lilliputian's goodies and hurried out of the hotel only five minutes late. I found Gilda waiting for me in front of the shop. A thick layer of North Texas dirt covered the glass door, but the inside was clean, if not a hint musty.

Two simple round racks sat in the middle of the store. A dress form was propped in the corner next to a large sewing machine and a rack of tools to rival any commercial sweatshop, holding everything from measuring tapes to buttonholers.

"Here, sugar, this rack is about the right formality for tonight," Gilda said. She flipped through the hanging clothes with a practiced hand, sliding hangers along the bar at a rapid pace. "Huh."

"Huh?"

"I thought we had more in a small size," she said.

"That's okay. I'm not that small."

"Well, most of these are for plus-sized women. I haven't had a chance to box them up yet like I have the others. We're donating to one of those shelters that helps women with interviews and such."

I joined her at the rack and did my own flip-through. The sizes didn't bother me as much as the style. They were everything a ninety-two-year-old woman living in the seventies would love. Lots of heavy polyester with scratchy panels and a hint of rosewater perfume.

"Here we go," Gilda said. "Two ideal choices. What luck!"

Luck indeed. A Gumby green floor length flared leg pantsuit with long sleeves and brass zipper right up the front or a striped sailor dress with one-inch pleats detailing the entire skirt. I thought of the silky black dress with matching slingbacks in the suitcase back in my hotel room. Pop star? Beauty queen? Barbie impersonator?

I sighed and accepted the dress as gracefully as I could. We paired it with a pair of red patent leather square-toed pumps that were only one size too small and left for the ball. If my outfit was any indication, I thought, this night is not going to go well.

EIGHT

We tooled toward the Broken Spoke in Gilda's flashy two-seater: a '60s VW Bug with the top securely up and arrived slightly past six on Friday evening. A stream of cars stretched from one side of the house, down the drive, and around the large oak while four tuxedoed valets hustled keys and escorted couples. Tall glass globes hung high above the path from the front walk to the side steps. Flower arrangements of bright pink peonies and orange lilies dotted the path. I saw the tops of party tents peeking through the trees and the rousing sounds of a country band floated over them.

The temperature had yet to sink a single degree as I emerged from the cool tin cocoon into a thick wall of heat. It had to be two hundred degrees. And apparently the Baron's Ball would be held in the backyard. Outside. In August. As Director of the Ballantyne, I'd often hosted outdoor events, but rarely the last week of August when the sun sizzled and scorched even the shadiest of spots. I avoided it not just for the comfort of our guests, but because nothing turned a party sour faster than a yard full of cranky donors with sticky clothes, fallen hairdos, and warm drinks.

But I'd never attended a summer event in Texas.

Large fans with ice misters hung from the tops of the poles blowing a cool breeze across a massive white tent in the very center of the backyard. Though "backyard" seemed to understate the grandness of the space. Perfectly manicured greens spread out like a city park, each side bordered with rose bushes and magnolia trees. Two smaller tents flanked the larger one with banquet tables arranged around intricately carved ice sculptures. I do believe actual air conditioners were placed around the perimeter. I could neither see them nor hear them, but the temperature beneath the billowy tents was twenty degrees cooler than the air just ten feet away.

Gilda and I went straight for the bar. Six different lemonade blends, nine varieties of iced tea, every soda ever created, and no less than ten flavors of Kool-Aid. But not a single drop of alcohol. I graciously accepted a cola martini. Gilda went off to find Rita and I went over to the main table.

Jolene Carter sat center with a group of women cooing about, offering their heartfelt Southern regrets at the passing of her father-in-law and the arrest of her mother-in-law.

"Why, you must be devastated, Jolene. Such a tragedy, here in your quaint little town," a woman said. She wore her big bleached hair tucked into an even bigger yellow hat.

"I know," another lady said. She was all a-dazzle in full-length pink sequins and a chunky pink stone necklace. "When I heard about your mama, I immediately ran right down here to see what I could get. I mean, get for you." She sipped something red from a frosty lemonade glass and smacked her lips. I wondered if she hadn't added a nip along the way.

Kathy Lee nudged the woman aside. "It's not her mama and you know it." She shooed away the small crowd. "You ladies go busy yourselves, dinner will be starting soon."

The woman in the yellow hat hugged Jolene half-heartedly with one arm, then started talking to her friends before she moved away. "I hope they serve the lobster," she said excitedly.

"It was ambrosia last year," another one said, her voice fading as they two-stepped toward a waiter passing a silver tray of canapés. "Let's sit at Wynonna's table. You know she caught her husband…"

"You might as well sit here, Elliott," Kathy Lee said. "Zibby's resting until Mama's ready. She won't be here for a spell yet and she'd twist my ear if I didn't extend you the courtesy. Even if you are wearing Shirley Temple's sailor suit. I thought you said you knew the dress code."

I ignored her and took a seat on the other side of the round table, setting my handbag on the chair next to mine, saving it for Zibby.

A short man in a ten gallon stunner approached the table. He placed a lime green drink in front of Jolene, then tipped his hat to me. "Ma'am. You must be this Elliott I keep hearing about. I'm Austin Carter the Second, but you can call me A.J. Everyone else does."

I introduced myself with a matching nod. "I'm truly sorry to hear about your father. He sounds like he was a kind man, and a favorite around here."

"Everyone loved Big Daddy," Jolene said.

"Well, clearly not everyone loved him," Kathy Lee said. "You getting closer to figuring this mess out, Elliott?"

I smiled and tried not to squirm. The heat made my feet swell and the too small shoes were beginning to pinch. "I am, actually. If you don't mind, I'd like to ask you all some questions before dinner."

A.J. interrupted before Kathy Lee could protest. "Go on, but I'm not sure what you can do that the sheriff can't."

"You know Mama's being railroaded by Bobby Wainwright," Kathy Lee said. "He's on a mission to slander the Carter name."

"Oh now, Kathy Lee, settle down," A.J. said. "Let's just get through the night without one of your hissy fits."

I took a sip of my fizzy Coke country martini and wished I had the foresight to buy a purse load of those little airline booze bottles while we were touring the friendly skies the night before. "Can you tell me about the will, A.J., since you're the attorney? The original one, before it was changed."

"Sure. But I didn't draw it up. Big Daddy had it done down in Dallas. Keep it fair. Basically all of Little Oak, property and land, went to both me and Kathy Lee, provided we settle on a project to support, and run, together. There's also a provision we take care of Mama and Broken Spoke."

"But he changed it after months of bickering," Jolene said. "Kathy Lee talking nonsense about a casino, when she knows full well this town's perfect for The Light of the Rock megachurch."

"Changed the will to what, exactly?" I asked.

A tuxedoed waiter began setting plates of greens in front of each diner. A.J. waited until he finished serving the table before answering. "If we couldn't agree on the town's new direction at the time of his death, then the entire package went to the Ballantyne Foundation."

Kathy Lee stabbed a cherry tomato and pointed it at me. "But he never intended to go through with it. And he's certainly spinning in his grave right now just listening to this horrifying turn of events."

Jolene dabbed her mouth with an ivory napkin. "Now *that* we agree on."

"Did the same provision stay with the new addendum?" I asked, ignoring them both. "The one where you're required to take care of Bea and the ranch?"

"Absolutely," A.J. said. "His first priority was Mama."

If Bea was financially cared for regardless of which way the will went, then there also went any financial motive for Bea killing her husband. "Did she take sides in the casino versus church debate? Maybe have a preference? Or was she maybe tired of the fighting in the family?"

"You ask a lot of questions for a charity worker," Bobby Wainwright said, approaching the table from behind me. "As the town's new owner, you starting your own police force?"

"You don't need a badge to ask questions," A.J. said.

"Around here you do," Bobby said.

"This is a private party, Bobby Wainwright," Kathy Lee said. "And you were not invited."

"Oh enough already, Kathy Lee," Jolene said, then smacked A.J. lightly on the arm. "You, too, sugar. He's already here, show some manners."

Bobby took off his cowboy hat and set it on the table, then sat two seats over from me.

"To answer your question," A.J. said pointedly to me, "Mama didn't prefer one project over the other."

"Mama didn't care for that pretend Indian chief one bit—"

"Mama hated that plastic preacher—"

A.J. raised his palms at Jolene and Kathy Lee and their simultaneous protests. "You know she supported us all, but did not want to be in the middle. And yes, she was definitely tired of the girls bickering night and day."

I was with Mama on that one. They were shredding my nerves like a block of hard cheese on a steel grater and I'd only been here one day. Can't imagine what it'd been like to live with those two round the clock. But it made more sense to knock one of them off, not their Big Daddy.

I tried to look as sheepish as I felt when I asked my next question. "Was Austin seeing someone on the side, perhaps?"

Kathy Lee threw down her fork and dressing splashed the tablecloth, but Jolene only laughed. "Sugar, even if he wanted to, which I assure you he certainly did not, he couldn't sneak anything in this town. Big Daddy was a walking bullhorn the size of Texas and every resident stopped to listen. Man never left the house or walked the square without someone in tow."

Two waiters approached the table. One cleared out salad dishes while the other replaced them with enormous dinner plates. I'm not sure I'd ever seen a single piece of beef so large. The first tender bite melted in my mouth like warm chocolate. It was paired with homemade bleu cheese mashed potatoes and I was hooked.

"So back to the will," I said between bites. "Who knew the terms?"

"Everyone within fifty miles at least," Bobby said. "I even knew about it and I haven't had a reason to visit Little Oak in years."

"You don't have one now," Kathy Lee added, then turned to me. "No one but the three of us and Mama knew about Big Daddy's ridiculous revision giving you the tiniest window to snatch away my birthright. So killing Big Daddy with it in place only made it worse for us."

I stuffed an overly large slice of steak into my mouth, forcing me to keep my pie hole shut. But we were thinking the same thing. The Ballantyne addendum pretty much ruled out the family's motive for murder. And opened everyone else in town up for scrutiny. Including the dashing preacher and the Indian chief. If they didn't know about the revision, then maybe they thought killing Big Daddy might tip the scales toward one project or the other.

Speaking of said preacher, I spotted him walking across the tent toward a table on the other side. He wore a sharp gray suit with a white cowboy hat. I was beginning to think cowboy hats were the number one reason the party was held outdoors, so all the men could wear them.

"Look at those flowers," Zibby said from behind me. "I've never seen a bloom so large!"

I turned just as she and Bea approached our table. Zibby looked not a day of her eighty-six years in a fuchsia ball gown and matching pillbox hat. She wore delicate lavender gloves, but I'm pretty sure they were inside out.

After a quick hug in greeting, I whispered in her ear about her gloves.

She eased into the chair next to mine and patted my hands. "I know, dear. This way they don't get dirty on the walk over." She took them off and stuck them under her hat.

"Mama, we were so worried about you," Jolene said. "Did they make you wear one of those dreadful orange jumpsuits? Did a gangbanger try to give you a beat down?"

"Seriously, Mama," Kathy Lee said. "Were you threatened? You didn't touch anything did you?"

"It was the local sheriff's lockup, girls," Bobby said. "She was booked, arraigned, bailed, and released in less than four hours. Didn't even sit in a cell."

"No thanks to you," Kathy Lee said. "I mean, she was there thanks to you."

Bea waved to a waiter and settled into her seat. She looked exhausted down to her soul. Dark circles and gray skin no amount of makeup could cover. "Bobby was very kind to rush things along. Sheriff and I had a nice visit on the way down, and Austin Jr. and I on the round trip. And I made it in time for the ball, so don't y'all be upset now."

"Mama, he arrested you for murderin' Big Daddy," Kathy Lee said. "Of course we're upset. We shouldn't have to sit with this scoundrel right at the table, at Daddy's party."

The waiter arrived with a frosty non-cocktail and steak dinner for each Bea and Zibby. As soon as they left, Bobby set his knife on the edge of his plate and picked up his hat. "Thank you, kindly, Miss Bea. I've long wanted to attend one of your Cattle Baron parties. If you'll excuse me, I best be on my way." He tipped his hat at Kathy Lee, then walked away.

"Really, Kathy Lee," Jolene said. "How you ever gonna lasso that man with that bad attitude of yours? He's waiting for you, circling the fences, and you keep throwing mud."

Kathy Lee just glared at her while A.J. looked confused.

I quickly hopped up and pulled Bobby aside.

"Can I ask you something?"

"Sure, long as it's not privy to the case," Bobby said.

"Why did you wait so long to arrest Bea? It's been nearly four weeks. Not to jump to conclusions, but you found her over the body, clutching the murder weapon, alone in the room."

He looked thoughtful a moment, as if trying to decide how much to share. "I guess it's no secret. I've known this family my whole life and Bea plain had no reason to kill Austin Sr. I stalled as long as I could, but folks in the D.A.'s office, the Sheriff's department, hell even here in Little Oak, started demanding answers. Couldn't deny the evidence in front of me even if I don't all the way believe it."

I thanked him and walked back to the table. Well, I guess that was everyone who doubted Bea killed Austin. Unfortunately doubts didn't do much until twelve of her peers shared them, too. Could be a long way from here to there and anything could happen.

Bea and Zibby had started an interesting conversation on the benefits of learning to rope cattle in kindergarten, so I decided to take a quick stroll around the tent, see what else I could dig up. I was one day down, less than two days until my departing flight, and no closer to finding Austin's killer than I was learning how to rope cattle.

I made excuses of needing a carbonated martini refill and a good leg stretch, then meandered amongst Little Oak's finest folks. Most women sparkled tip to toe. Glitzy jewelry and sequined dresses. Even their hats were bedazzled. The country band had added at least four new members and couples started lighting up the dance floor.

Whoever killed Austin Carter was likely at the ball. Celebrating? Did his death benefit them or must they now deal with the fallout of an unexpected addendum to his will?

I noticed Gilda Hays and Rita Whitaker enjoying the party. Funny how every other business in the square closed, but theirs stayed open. And their businesses at the end of Main Street showed no signs of closing.

Then I spotted the Reverend and the Chief huddled together just one table over. Neither benefitted from the Ballantyne addendum, but they couldn't have known about it when Austin died. Maybe one of them hoped with Austin gone, they could gain more ground?

I casually looped a wide arc around the back side of the tent, balancing between staying inside the cool air and blending into the crowd. I quietly slipped into a chair behind the huddle.

"Doesn't seem...really going to be...on the way..." Reverend Kincaid said in a voice so low I barely heard him.

"...she'll take care...our time next...confident for the..." Chief Fannin replied.

I leaned back, tipped my head at the oddest of angles, but still couldn't make out every fourth word. Seems I wasn't going to be able to eavesdrop, though just noticing these two plotting was suspicious enough. They could be simply talking about the weather, but I didn't think so. I strained one last time and nearly slipped off my chair. I decided I better join them before I crashed into them.

"Oh hello, Chief Fannin, Reverend Kincaid," I said. "Nice to see you again. May I sit a moment? I'm afraid my feet are killing me." Not an untrue statement. I was tempted to kick off my shoes under the table except I'd never get those suckers back on.

"Of course, red-headed woman," the Chief said.

"It's auburn, actually," I said. "I didn't realize you two were friends. Or is this you keeping your enemies closer?"

The Reverend chuckled good-naturedly. "Elliott, right? Chief Fannin and I go back more than ten years. We've worked several charity events together."

"Indeed," Chief Fannin replied. "Our people are a giving people. We believe in returning the benefits given to us. Unlike you who has chosen to take away from Little Oak."

"Let's not be too hard on her," Reverend Kincaid said. "She's just doing her job."

"Maybe she needs a new job," Chief Fannin said. "One with a higher moral standard."

"Sounds like she's only following the path set before her. Takes a strong woman to lead a charitable foundation."

I tried not to preen at the compliment as I quietly listened as these two played good cop, bad cop, bantering about my life's work. The Ballantynes treated me like family, had since I was a young girl, and working at their foundation was a dream for me. Sometimes the crazy kind of dream where bananas talked and my telephone doubled as a washing machine, but a dream all the same.

The preacher and the chief finally paused long enough for me to get a word in. "I'm sorry to contradict you gentlemen, but the Ballantyne truly is a reputable organization, and the will donating Little Oak is legally sound," I said.

"The court will have plenty to say about that," Chief Fannin said. "My people do not fear fighting for their lands."

"I've never heard of the Big Spring Choctaw before," I said. "I did a little research. Not much out there."

"You researched our tribe?" He looked affronted, but not the embarrassment I expected if he had been hiding something. "When? On the way to the party?"

"We have a very thorough research staff at the Ballantyne," I said. And we usually did. My lack of a laptop and Tod's puppy baby shower duties notwithstanding. "We found little information on your tribe."

"Our people prefer a less recognized lifestyle," Chief Fannin said. "Unlike your Ballantyne which draws attention to itself weekly."

Now it was my turn to look affronted—and embarrassed. I worked hard to keep those headlines positive and infrequent. I'm not always successful.

"Elliott, we would love to have you attend our revival tomorrow," Reverend Kincaid said. He smiled and leaned forward on the table. "The Light of the Rock congregation will be celebrating the Lord's goodness. It might change your mind about things. From one charitable organization to another."

"And our rally, too," Chief Fannin said, not to be left out. "The Big Spring Choctaw tribe will be celebrating the wealth of the land as well."

The more I listened, the more they seemed like the type to simply take their show on the road, work their charm in the next town. They were already shifting their attitude with me, trying to work me to join one of their groups.

"I think I shall. Stop by to both, I mean," I said.

Coffee service began and I said my good evenings. They immediately huddled back up with low voices. No one else seemed to think it suspicious, so what did I know? I really only did have less than ten percent of my PI hours logged. Not like I knew what I was doing.

However, when did the Chief research the Ballantyne? That day, like me, huddled over a sketchy cell connection, or earlier. And how much earlier? Something tickled my memory, but I couldn't figure out what.

I hopped one table over just as thick slices of strawberry cake with rich pink frosting arrived.

"Elliott, you look adorable in that dress," Gilda said. "I knew it was perfect."

I sank into one of the empty chairs, ridiculously comfortable for a banquet chair. I was beginning to think I could learn something from these Texas party planners.

"Yes, a perfect dress," I lied. "You totally saved me. But these shoes might kill me."

Rita passed me a decadent piece of cake. "This will cure it. One bite and you'll forget all about your feet."

She was right. It was silky and sweet with a hint of tart from the crisp berries on top. I could've eaten five slices of that cake in one sitting.

"You coming to the groundbreaking tomorrow?" Gilda asked me.

"Only one? I thought both the sinners and the saints had something going on," I said.

"They do," Rita said. "Officially, they are both hosting celebrations tomorrow to get all the folks ramped up. Then the groundbreakings are next week."

"Even though only one project will go forward?" I asked. "Won't that be costly for one of the groups?"

"Yep," Gilda said. "But the Carter girls are convinced their own project will win, so neither will back down."

"Well, I know the casino will easily gain more favor with residents," Rita said. She sat back and sipped her coffee. "But since either project will take at least a year to build, better to get started now."

"It really will be spectacular tomorrow," Gilda said. "You'll be glad you're here. Town's lucky to get either one."

I ate the last bite of cake and pondered this predicament. A religious retreat and a gambling hall aren't exactly the types of establishments the Ballantyne Foundation usually supports. Nothing wrong with either, really, but neither seemed in need of charitable assistance. We generally tended to the struggling, the educational, environmental, and social organizations in need of financial generosity. "Mr. Ballantyne would never approve of either project," I said.

"Can I quote you on that?"

I jerked around at the sound of a familiar weasely voice. "Absolutely not," I said.

"Tate Keating, reporter for the Islander Post," he said to the table. He had a notebook in one hand and a pen in the other. He wore a brown plaid shirt with the cuffs turned back and a leather bowtie. All very Jimmy Olsen goes to the rodeo.

"What are you doing here in Texas?" I asked, irritated his eavesdropping efforts might be more successful than mine and net him another jazzy headline.

"Chasing a scandalous story, Elliott," Tate said. "You wouldn't return my calls, so I hopped on a plane to check things out myself."

"Return your calls! Tate, I left you three messages," I said. "There is nothing here for you to see. The Carters graciously donated Little Oak to the Ballantyne, and I'm here to thank them. No scandal, no drama. Just routine charity stuff."

"That's not what I hear," he said in a singsong voice and merrily waved his notebook.

"Well, you heard wrong. You leave these fine folks alone," I said with a shooing hand motion. "This is an invitation-only party and you were not on the list."

He looked around the table one last time, hoping for a little juice, but Rita and Gilda sat silent. "Fine by me. But wait until you see Sunday's headline. Going to be a grabber!"

Heat rose up my back and I felt my cheeks flush bright red. Tate Keating made newspaper mountains out of mole hills, always searching for his ticket out of a small town island paper. Guess he thought the Ballantyne would pay the fare.

I stood and watched him walk across the tent. He turned back once and gave me a small finger wave, then ducked out along the lighted path. I stared at the path for a full minute, in case he returned. The only person I saw was an elderly woman in a maid's uniform enter the side door to the house.

"I'm going to make sure Tate's left the grounds," I said. "You guys staying awhile?"

"Oh at least a half hour, I'd say," Gilda said.

"You need a ride back to the inn?" Rita asked. "I'm happy to take you. I need one more cup of coffee in me, then I'll be ready."

"Perfect," I said, then limped away. If I didn't lose the shoes soon, my feet might cramp forever.

I used the same side entrance as the maid and entered a long mudroom with built-in cabinets running the length of each wall. It was brightly lit and several servers passed by me carrying coffee carafes and the final trays of cake. I followed the sound of clinking glass through an enormous commercial kitchen where a mostly college-aged staff diligently washed and packed stacks of china. No one questioned me as I entered the main house. I don't think anyone even noticed.

Kathy Lee, or Jolene, I couldn't remember, mentioned Austin's study was at the back of the house, along with the maid's quarters, so I stuck to the rear rooms. Beautiful dark wood floors gleamed in the lamplight while plush decorative rugs muffled my clomping footsteps. I found it hard to walk stealthily with my throbbing feet jammed into plastic pumps.

I passed two powder rooms (taking a quick detour to make use of one of the lovely facilities), a sitting room, and an enormous hall decorated with a pair of ranch scene oil paintings, each larger than freeway billboard. Two mahogany and glass doors flanked a room at the opposite end. Even without the gaudy crime scene tape, I knew it was the study. A piece of heavy carpet had been cut from the rest, near the center of the room.

The walls were covered in hand-carved bookshelves, stained dark like the doors. Silk-shaded wall sconces bathed the room in a soft light. An imposing desk sat off to one side. Typical executive accessories graced the top: an antique lamp, a fancy pen and pencil set in personalized holder, and a matching brass letter opener and scissor set.

I was about to check out the credenza when I realized what I'd seen. I reached out and picked them up. Brass scissors. Not unusual, since most executives probably have a similar set somewhere in their office. But considering Austin was killed with a pair of scissors, and his were sitting pretty on his desk, then it followed the killer brought their own pair.

"Strange isn't it?" a small voice said from behind me.

I jumped back and accidentally whipped the sharp scissors into the visitor's chair. They stood perfectly straight, tips firmly planted in a needlepoint pillow. I quickly picked it up and apologized to the elderly woman in the doorway.

She smiled, but didn't move. She kept her feet firmly on the wood outside the study, her toes an inch from the carpet.

"No worries, now," she said softly. "Miss Bea has dozens of those old pillahs. Been stitchin' 'em since she was a kitten."

"You must be Mrs. Alden," I said gently.

Her maid's uniform hung loose on her tiny frame. But it was starched stiff and would pass any military inspection.

"Indeed. Been with the family muh whole life. Now you come on out of there. Nothing good in that room." She turned and very slowly walked into the large hall.

I realized I was still holding the stabbed pillow, the scissors jutting from the center. A grim reenactment of the recent events. I quickly pulled out the scissors, returned them to their holder on the desk, and the pillow to the chair, and rushed from the room.

Mrs. Alden waited for me on a settee beneath one of the oil paintings.

"Mr. Austin painted these himself, you know. Oh, 'bout thirty years, I guess now. Took him two years to finish each one. Was a talent."

I studied the one across from us and realized the ranch depicted in broad strokes was the Broken Spoke in the spring. The house was in the background, a squat barn and horse ring in the foreground.

"They're beautiful," I said.

"He loved this ranch more than anything. Except Miss Bea, of course. Loved this town, too."

"It must have been awful finding him that way. Finding them both, really."

She pulled a tattered tissue from her front pocket and gripped it in her fragile hand. Her skin was covered in large dark spots, her veins as visible as her knuckles.

"Horrible. Worst night of my eight-seven years. And I've had some nights."

"Do you think Miss Bea was to blame?" I asked as gently as I could. I wasn't sure how she would answer such a bold question from a stranger, but this woman had been behind the scenes of the Carter clan for almost a century. If anyone knew the scoop, it was Mrs. Alden.

"Absolutely not. Makes no sense, now. I'm only tellin' you because I know who you are and you're here to help. Help Miss Bea, maybe even help those two girls who can't get out of their own way."

"It doesn't make sense to me either. I don't know the Carters, but seeing the scissors on his desk changes things. Who would bring scissors to meet with Austin?"

"Must have been some pretty important scissors."

"I'm sure the police have asked you many times, but did you hear anyone in the house that night, maybe an argument?"

She tapped her right ear and said, "Perfect hearing, but my room's through the parlor down that hall. And this house's built like she looks, strong and thick. I wouldn't have heard much unless they was screaming something fierce."

"Did you let someone in, a visitor, maybe earlier in the evening, and they stayed late?"

"The Carters didn't entertain for dinner that night. Miss Bea went up to bed right after." Mrs. Alden patted my leg. "Which was normal for them. Miss Bea's getting on in years, gets sleepy after a nip of wine with her meal."

"And Austin?"

"Mr. Austin took meetings all day and sometimes late into the night. Had an open door policy. Said he needed to, what with owning the town and all." She pointed to a door to our left, about ten feet from the study. An outer door by the looks of it. "Doorbell rings low in the study only. Whole town knows they can ring it anytime. If Mr. Austin's still up, he'll answer."

She sighed deep, and I bet she felt it in her soul. "If only he'd gone up with Miss Bea."

I helped her to her feet and we slowly shuffled down the hall toward her room. "Thank you, Mrs. Alden. You've been very kind to answer my questions."

She gripped my hand, tighter than I thought her capable. "You help Miss Bea, now. These're good people."

I assured her I would, and walked back through the kitchen and out the side door. While Mrs. Alden didn't tell me anything I didn't already know or suspect, she did say one thing that stuck with me the rest of the night.

"Must have been some pretty important scissors."

Indeed.

NINE

I awoke hot and hungry and not at all rested. I was less than twenty-four hours from an unknown headline guaranteed to rattle Mr. Ballantyne five countries over, Zibby looked one hot flash away from a heart attack when we said our goodnights after the party, and I felt certain if I didn't help Bea Carter quickly, the wheels of justice would ride her right into her own grave. So far I wasn't living up to my investigative potential in Little Oak and I was due back on Sea Pine Island tomorrow.

Which reminded me of my luggage. I dragged out of bed and nearly knocked over the beautiful bottle of whiskey on the nightstand. I'd moved it closer to the bed in a moment of temptation the night before. If I ever needed a nip, it was last night. I held off, but if today didn't improve, I may end up in the corner with a glass in one hand and the bottle of booze in the other.

I sat on the edge of the chair and dialed the airline. My call was quickly answered with the same recording as before. Storms, claims, delays, blah blah blah. I glanced at the heavy Texas tee balled up in the corner and decided I'd rather hold than smother myself in that blanket again. Soothing music drifted over the line. Something designed to keep me distracted, no doubt. And it did. Took me ten minutes to remember the name of the song. *Torn Between Two Lovers*, the instrumental version. I studied my swollen feet. Two toe blisters and an ugly red indentation on the back of my left heel. I checked my watch for the seventeenth time. Still holding, still getting the blah blah blah, still starving. And now ridiculously late. I clicked the end button and stood. Time to shake it off and take action.

I marched over to the suitcase and carefully checked it on the slimmest possibility I'd somehow overlooked all of my things the day before. Or perhaps some of the pieces weren't as tiny as I remembered.

I lifted out a soft (clean) black tee and sighed with envy. I wouldn't fit into that minikin no matter how desperate I was. Two papers fluttered out. The name Jaya Jones was inlaid on the first sheet, a handwritten letter, and the other looked like a historical document, worn and mysterious, written in faded brown ink, protected by a plastic sheet. Tucked beside them was a magnifying glass. British detective? Treasure seeker? Egyptian excavator?

I closed the lid with a snap. Nothing inside to help me with my wardrobe deficiency.

But I still had the glamorous gumshoe's shower products. I ducked into the bathroom and emerged twenty minutes later feeling refreshed, renewed, and ready to kick some Texas barbeque butt in my own clothes. I had washed my tee in the shower and dried it with the hair dryer. It was wrinkled and wine-stained, but clean.

First order for the morning was to call Bobby Wainwright and ask about those scissors. His office was closed.

Right, it was Saturday. I left a message in case he checked in and I hoped I'd run into him in town.

I slid into my flip flops and went straight down to the dining room. It was packed as if Rita was topping every biscuit with hundred dollar bills. The air buzzed with excitement, smiles on every face, and chatter so loud, I could no longer hear my own stomach grumble.

After some minor elbowing and firm nudging, I managed to score the remnants of a blueberry scone with a tab of butter. I carried my bounty to the lobby and sat on the only vacant spot: the stairs.

"Good morning, Elliott. Today is the day!" Rita said. She practically bounced she was so jubilant. "Haven't had a full house like this in five years easy."

"All this for the revival?"

"And the casino rally." Rita fluffed her big hair as she bustled around the front desk. "Chief Fannin's expecting more than three hundred folks today. Once we open the doors to the casino, I'll never have a vacant room again. I've got to run, set up's been going on since dawn, party's gonna start any second. You come on by, see what we've got, you hear?"

"Wouldn't miss it." And I wouldn't. Or the revival. The answer to the puzzle had to lie within those two tents.

I brushed the crumbs from my fingers and tossed my napkin in the trash bin, then made my way outside. Brilliant sunshine glared from the bright blue sky. It had to be at least one hundred degrees out, maybe even hotter, with the heat radiating from the brick pavers. But that didn't slow anyone down. The town looked like I'd imagined it would when Zibby first described it.

Packs of families walked down the sidewalks and up the middle of the road. There must have been some sort of shuttle system because there wasn't a single car in the town square. Several people rode bicycles and scooters, slowly weaving through the foot traffic. I joined the lively crowd and their enthusiasm propelled me through the town.

Balloon clusters in bright reds, yellows, and blues surrounded a banner on the left tent, declaring "The Broken Spoke Casino Welcomes You!" Jazzy sounds of the Rat Pack era rocked the tent, as Frank Sinatra asked that luck please be a lady. Two petite dark-skinned women, both with long shiny black hair, in full suede-fringed and turquoise regalia greeted visitors as they entered the tent.

On the right side of the road, glittery gold fabric draped a shimmering white tent, its banner inviting people to the Light of the Rock Revival. A chorus of gospel sang out for the good Lord to abide with us, and from the glorious robust voices, I imagined no less than one hundred gowned singers assembled inside, hands raised, bodies swaying.

A long swath of wide red ribbon graced the front of each opposing tent, about twenty feet from their entrances, close to the road.

I debated which event to join first, rally or revival, when the decision was made for me. The sweet smoky aroma of Texas barbeque wafted over me from the center of town. It smelled juicy and tangy and my feet started walking before my brain said go.

I spotted Gilda manning a tented station filled with metal trays of hickory smoked beef, baked beans, fried macaroni and cheese, and some kind of corn slaw with red peppers. Bakery fresh buns were stacked blacktop to tent top and large squeeze bottles of sauces in varying shades of red lined the front table.

"You've never tasted something so good, Elliott," Gilda said, meeting me in front. "You thought our restaurant barbeque was divine, wait until you taste it streetside."

Gilda piled a plate high for me while I grabbed a glass of raspberry iced tea. "I may faint from the savory smell alone," I said.

I followed her to a nearby picnic table in the middle of the road, square between both tents. Gilda handed me a stack of napkins, then tucked some under her chin to protect her shirt: a white tee with "Light of the Rock" spelled out in flowing script above a metallic gold cross.

One bite of my barbeque beef sandwich and I moaned out loud. A burst of sweet and spicy sauce mixed with the tender smoky meat, and the soft buttery bun wrapped the whole delightful package like gourmet birthday present. I'll say this about Texas, they sure know how to cook meat.

"Aren't these types of festivities usually reserved for a grand opening?" I asked. "Especially since they want to tear down the entire town?"

"Maybe folks figure they better do it now before the Ballantyne comes in and takes over," Gilda said.

"Good morning, y'all," Jolene said from behind me. "Isn't this the most glorious day? Praise the Lord, He certainly shining down us today!"

Jolene walked up with the Carter clan: A.J., Kathy Lee, and Bea, with Zibby slowly bringing up the rear. Jolene and A.J. wore the same white church tees as Gilda, while Kathy Lee sported a brown and red Broken Spoke Casino tee. Bea and Zibby had abstained.

"Jolene, for once we agree," Kathy Lee said. "I do believe the Lord is giving the Big Spring Choctaw and the Broken Spoke Casino His blessing."

Gilda quickly made up plates for the group and served them at our table with fresh pitchers of tea. "Elliott here was just asking about the festivities," she said when she returned. "Wanted to know why the fuss so early."

"The Ballantyne's ownership aside, seems you'd celebrate after the construction, not before," I said.

"We do things big in Texas," Jolene said.

"Yes, indeedy," Gilda agreed. "And the Worship Center is going to do Texas proud. So big, you might see it from space. We'll seat fifteen thousand per service."

"That's just ridiculous," Kathy Lee said. "Couldn't fill it full in a month of Sundays. You two refuse to listen to me. The casino will allow Little Oak to thrive."

"If Joel Osteen can do it in Houston, then we can, too. We're close enough to Dallas," Jolene said.

Reverend Kincaid might be a charmer, I thought, but he's no Joel Osteen. I turned to Bea who sat at the far end of the table, facing the ranch. She looked thoughtful, closely following the debate, as if hearing it for the first time.

"Which project is better for the town, Bea?" I asked.

"The Ballantyne, probably. My girls are passionate, God bless them, but this has torn the family right down the middle." Her eyes filled with tears and she pushed away her plate. "I know Austin only wanted to pressure them into deciding, but I maybe his death might bring a silver lining."

"Now Mama, don't be morbid," Kathy Lee said. "Nothing good about Daddy dying or that charity taking over his heritage."

Jolene got up and hugged Bea tight. "You're always looking for the bright side, Mama Bea. You're an angel. We're going to build a special place for you right up front of the church."

"Stop it, Jolene," Kathy Lee said. "Always trying to push yourself onto everyone else. Let the woman be. She's got a lot to deal with now, running the ranch herself."

"Not alone, Kathy Lee," A.J. piped in. "Stop being so melodramatic."

"It's not melodrama, it's reality," Kathy Lee said. "That ranch doesn't run for free. That's why the casino project makes the most sense."

"The Lord's riches are worth more than the Earth's," Jolene said.

"Well, the Lord created the Earth, so I'm pretty sure it's all the same," Kathy Lee snapped back.

Gilda and Rita both rose and moved behind their respective friends as Kathy Lee and Jolene faced off in the center of town.

"Money won't get you into heaven," Jolene said. "You only offer money, we offer salvation."

"I'll make the money and work out my own salvation," Kathy Lee said. "You don't own a corner on getting into heaven just because you want to build a church."

"Better than your sin palace," Jolene said.

Bobby Wainwright entered the tight circle with the sheriff right next to him. They gently pushed between the two women.

"Seems you ladies know how to gather a crowd," Bobby said. "Though I don't think this is what you had in mind. More like making a spectacle."

I glanced around. Looked like most folks were drifting from the tents and edging closer to the scene in the street. Chief Fannin and his counterpart from across the divide slowly joined the party. The Chief wore feathers on his brown vest while I'd swear the Reverend wore glitter in his hair.

Bea and Zibby stood, as did I, since my view was now completely obstructed from the seated position. I followed behind them, figuring they'd get in the middle of the circle. I was right.

"This stops here, right now" Bea said. "You two have graduated from splitting our family to splitting the whole town." She waved to the sea of people, half on one side, half on the other. "It's to the point everyone's taking sides. No matter which way it goes now, we'll only please half and os-tracize the rest."

Zibby moved in close, then wobbled, and I feared she was about to topple over from the heat. Instead she wiped her brow with a saucy napkin, then handed it to the sheriff. "Why don't you do both?" she asked. "Build a casino on one side and the church on the other. Then everyone will be hap-py."

I laughed. Well, more like an unladylike guffaw. "Sure, the sinners can make money at night, then be saved in the morning."

"That's a lovely idea, Zibby," Bea said and gave her a squeeze. "And it solves everything."

Jolene grabbed the Reverend's arm. "We can host ser-vices nearly every day of the week. Fill those seats faster than Joel Osteen does."

"Wait, what?" I said. "What about the Ballantyne?"

"And with the draw from the megachurch," Kathy Lee added, smiling for the first time since I met her, "we'll get nearly double the traffic in the casino."

Gilda joined the hoopla and her joyous grin made her look like a kid heading to Disneyland. "Now we can stay open. The inn, the restaurant and my gift shop! Isn't that the best news, Rita? And we can bring back the Honeysuckle Festival, with a few adjustments, of course."

"I never planned on leaving," Rita said. "Figured Little Oak would open up once Ballantyne finally got here, but this is even better."

She was the first, and only, person to acknowledge the Ballantyne. And from the moment I arrived. She was welcoming and expecting me, even with all the party planning. The tickle in my memory finally popped: the Honeysuckle banner she ordered months ago. How many months ago, I wondered. Before Austin's death?

"How did you know you'd be staying?" I asked. "You printed up the Honeysuckle Festival banner, even though it had been cancelled long ago."

"I figured the Ballantyne would bring back the shops and the festival. I read up on Mr. Ballantyne and knew he'd never approve of the casino or the church. Even talked to that reporter from the Islander Post. He agreed. Said he'd just attended a glitzy tea party for sick children you hosted, and those are the Ballantyne's favorite causes."

"The Wonderland Tea was held early this year," Zibby said, referring to our annual tea party for terminally ill children.

"More than six weeks ago, as a matter of fact," I said. "A solid two weeks before Austin Carter was murdered. How did you know about the Ballantyne's involvement before I did?"

"Why, I told her. We've been best friends since child-hood," Kathy Lee said. She looked worried, her brow wrinkled and her smile long faded. "I don't understand what's going on."

The crowd parted as Rita inched backward and I saw the Light of the Rock tent behind her. And the bright red ribbon fluttering slowly in the wind. The same ribbon I saw in the living room lobby yesterday morning. For the ribbon cutting. Takes a pretty important pair of scissors to cut such thick and special ribbon.

I quickly turned to Bobby and the sheriff. "The scissors, from Austin's chest." I reached over and squeezed Bea's arm in apology. "Were they overly large, like you'd use for a ribbon cutting?"

"Yes, ma'am," Bobby said. "About a foot long and solid brass."

"Oh my Lord," Gilda said. "I didn't even make the connection, I've been so caught up in the sinner versus saints war. We're missing a pair of scissors. Rita and I put out the supplies this morning. We had matched pairs, long and gold and sharp enough to slice a tin can, but one was gone from the box. I had to run grab my sewing shears instead."

"Rita, you were in charge of the party supplies," Jolene said. "I personally delivered the boxes to your office back in June. Both scissors were there, I saw them."

Rita froze, stuck in place as everyone stared at her, waiting for an answer. And everyone included the Carters, the prosecutor, the sheriff, and the hundred or so people crowding around.

"It's…it's…" she stuttered. "It wasn't like that." She looked over her shoulder toward the church tent, then her eyes darted over the people in the street. She was starting to panic, trapped like a witch in Salem while everyone held a burning torch.

"It wasn't like what?" Kathy Lee looked horrified. "Are you saying you killed my Daddy?"

"No, no…not really. It wasn't fair," she said in a weak voice.

Bobby put his arm around Kathy Lee and her strong demeanor began to crumble. She leaned in to him with his hand firmly on her waist.

"Daddy treated you like family," Kathy Lee said. "Like one of his daughters."

"One of his daughters?" Rita choked out. "He offered me the same exact amount of money as everyone else in the square. Even that ditz who only owned that mystic beads shop for two years. Two years! I've been here my whole life. Given my life to this town. His town. And he's just going to shut me down? Shut us all down?"

She turned to Gilda for support, but she moved away to stand with Bea and her family.

"I tried to reason with Austin," Rita said. "Show him the inn could be valuable to either project, but he refused. Said it was up to his family, not the townsfolk. He called me townsfolk! I've stuck by your bitchy, stuck up, nasty side for thirty-five years, Kathy Lee. Thirty-five years! And he called me townsfolk." She practically spit out the last word, full of bitterness and resentment.

"So you figured the only way to keep the inn was for the Ballantyne to take it over," I said.

"It's *my* inn!" she screamed, her fists balled at her sides. "No one's taking it over. Why can't you see that! I was the only one willing to fight for what's mine. And I got it!"

"I'm not so sure about that," the sheriff said and reached behind him.

And with that, she ran.

Which was hard to do surrounded by a crowd with the sheriff and the prosecutor standing two feet away. But she tried. She pushed three people to the ground and shot through the opening behind her. Straight into the red ribbon in front of the Light of the Rock.

TEN

Zibby and I spent the rest of the afternoon splitting our time between the Light of the Rock Revival and the Broken Spoke Casino Rally. They both turned out to be quite entertaining, considering the morning's events. Bobby stayed by Kathy Lee's side all day, helping her cope, and host, and I think she may have even smiled again.

Jolene practically glowed as she and A.J. worshipped and welcomed new flock into their fold. And Miss Bea's cheeks finally got their color back, in direct proportion with getting her family, and her town, back.

Gilda took over the Little Oak Inn temporarily while the law handled Rita Whitaker. Rita made a formal confession to the sheriff on the ride down to Dallas. Told him the entire tragedy and then never stopped talking. I guess once she got on her self-righteous soapbox, sharing her outrage at her situation and limited choices, she never stepped down.

It didn't take too much persuading to convince Mr. Ballantyne to return Little Oak to the Carter family. Especially since it was Zibby's idea. Probably take another year to make it through the legal system, but he gave his word to Miss Bea and it was settled.

With four hours to go before my return flight to Sea Pine Island, I took my final shower in the tiny bathroom with an invigorating mix of alternating hot and cold water and dressed in my wine-stained tee and paisley skirt. I'd laundered the entire outfit plus the I Heart Texas shirt in the sink the night before. I am nothing if not clean.

I placed the Texas tee on the bed next to the items from Jaya the Explorer's belongings. I carefully re-folded every item, neatly placing outfits in short stacks. Or at least how I'd coordinate them. Then using a box of Ziplocs I'd borrowed from Gilda, I packaged up all of her wet goods, then re-packed the entire suitcase, including the beautiful bottle of Kentucky whiskey. I must admit I was quite proud of myself for not breaking into the bottle over the last two days. Lastly, I stuck the I Heart Texas tee on top along with a quickly penned letter.

With two snaps to the suitcase latches, I left the Little Oak Inn and met Zibby on the sidewalk out front. I took a last look around town. It was quite a whirlwind weekend and I'd never eaten so much meat in all my life. I remembered the delightful barbeque sauce and thought I might just have to come back here and do it again someday.

Dear Jaya,

It seems the airline switched our suitcases and I must apologize for rifling through your belongings. Though I was tempted to adorn myself with your adventurer's garb, I refrained. Mostly because I couldn't possibly squeeze myself into your tiny wardrobe or your enviable miniature shoes. I did, though, indulge in your shower products, but desperate times call for desperate measures, and my suitcase-switched twin, I found myself with barely a thin bar of soap in a dusty wrapper, and a girl can only handle so much. Please accept this fashionable Texas tee as thank you for your unwitting hospitality. I hope you're off at a photo shoot in Zanzibar or on safari in Tanzania, while I'm headed to my quiet island home. Maybe our paths will cross one day.

Yours sincerely,
Elliott Lisbon

PART 3:
FOOL'S GOLD

A Jaya Jones Treasure Hunt Mystery Novella (prequel to *Artifact*)

by Gigi Pandian

ONE

I stepped onto the stage of the theater. The spotlight blinded me, but after a few seconds my eyes began to adjust. The stage was nearly empty. To my left, a wooden wardrobe cabinet. To my right, a weathered whisky barrel that had seen better days. Rows of plush red seats stretched out in the dark theater, all of them vacant.

"You look awful, Jaya." The voice filled the air, but I remained alone.

I whipped around, looking from the seats to the rafters to the wings, only to be confronted with emptiness. The backstage area had been empty as well, which is why I was now standing here in search of Sanjay.

A moment later, he appeared on the stage a few feet away from me. From where, exactly, I can't be sure. Sanjay is a magician. The Hindi Houdini. A bowler hat sat on his head, as usual, but today his outfit was a black t-shirt and jeans instead of the tuxedo he usually wore when performing.

"Nice to see you, too," I said.

"I thought you were a good traveler."

"You try being delayed at the Dallas airport for eight hours, then arriving in Edinburgh to find you ended up with someone else's suitcase."

"That explains your ridiculous clothing," Sanjay said. "I thought this magic cabinet had transported me back to 1980."

"Very funny." I smoothed out the florescent pink Edinburgh Fringe Festival t-shirt I was wearing, wondering whether I should have borrowed some of the vintage 1960s clothing I'd found in the suitcase that wasn't mine. It was definitely much more stylish. "At least the night clerk at the hotel was nice enough to open the hotel gift shop at 3 a.m. so I could grab a t-shirt and leggings. This t-shirt was the only thing that came remotely close to fitting. I left my clothes from the flight with the hotel's laundry service."

"I'm surprised you didn't go shopping this morning."

"I chose sleep." I yawned.

"Now that I'm getting used to it," Sanjay said, looking me up and down, "it's not so bad. I don't think I've ever seen you in pink before. Come to think of it, I don't think I've seen you in anything besides black or gray."

"What about you? No tuxedo? I thought you liked to practice your show in full attire."

"It's not even noon."

"I know," I said. "I should still be sleeping."

Sanjay grinned. "Thanks for coming."

"Sanjay!" A voice with a thick Scottish accent called out from under the stage. "What's the hold up?"

"My friend Jaya's here," Sanjay called back.

A stagehand materialized on the stage next to Sanjay. As had been the case with Sanjay, I'm not sure from where he appeared.

Auburn curls stuck out around the edges of an orange ski cap. "So you're Jaya Jones," the stagehand said. "Sanjay was all broken up that your flight didn't make it in time for you to have dinner with him last night. Can't say I blame him. I'm Ewan."

Sanjay's face flushed as I shook Ewan's hand. I don't know why. Of course it was too bad I couldn't make it on time as planned and was instead relegated to a twenty-four-hour journey from San Francisco to Edinburgh due to bad-weather delays.

I'd only met Sanjay two months before, but he was one of those people who immediately felt like family. He was the best friend I'd made in San Francisco since moving there for my first university teaching job. I finished my PhD in history earlier in the year after completing the research for my dissertation at the British Library in London.

When Sanjay told me he was performing a magic show at the Edinburgh Fringe Festival, the largest performing arts festival in the world that takes place each August, I knew it was fate—or at least an excellent opportunity. A friend from when I lived in London was also going to be at the festival.

This was going to be a perfect vacation. Flight delays and switched luggage aside, I was ready to enjoy my first real vacation in ages. I'd spent the summer preparing for the four undergraduate history courses I'd be teaching that fall, and I desperately needed a break. I had two weeks before the semester started. I was going to spend this week in Edinburgh relaxing, doing a little sightseeing, and enjoying the festival.

I might have had an ulterior motive as well. I was getting over a break-up. I deserved this treat before diving into real life.

Sanjay narrowed his eyes at the stagehand and cleared his throat. "The show opens tonight," he said, his face slowly returning to normal color. "I'm still working out the kinks of my biggest illusion, so I don't have time to take a break right now. We need to do a full run-through with light and sound as soon as the other member of the crew arrives."

"Do you need any help?" I asked.

"You'd be up for helping?"

"Why not? I've got a little time."

"There's one thing," Sanjay said hesitantly. He pointed to a section of seats close to the stage. "Take a seat in the front on the left, and watch the stage carefully. That's my weak spot. I think I've got it fixed, but I haven't done an audience test yet. Ewan is helping from backstage—"

"Below-stage," Ewan said, "if you want to be accurate." He winked at me.

"The point being that you can't see the illusion from the proper vantage point," Sanjay said.

"Fair enough," Ewan said. "You sure you want her to help?"

"Why wouldn't I help?" I asked.

Ewan shrugged before walking off stage.

"What did he mean by that?" I asked Sanjay.

He gave a non-committal shrug suspiciously similar to Ewan's, and didn't meet my gaze when he spoke. "Who knows?"

"I'm ready whenever you are," Ewan called out, his voice below us.

I jumped down from the stage and sat in the first row.

"Who," Sanjay began in a booming theatrical voice, "would like to help me ensure the integrity of this illusion? If the lovely lady in the first row with shoulder-length black hair and dangerous heels would assist me?"

I rolled my eyes and hopped back on stage.

"Have we ever met before?" Sanjay asked.

"You can skip the banter," I said. "There's nobody in the audience."

Sanjay sighed. Even the sigh was an overdone theatrical sigh. "Don't you know anything about rehearsing?" he asked.

"Fine." I said. "I don't know you, and am not your confederate."

"Thank you. Now, please select one of the following implements to tie my wrists behind my back."

He lifted a black cloth from the top of the whisky barrel, revealing two types of handcuffs and three kinds of rope. He moved the objects of restraint from the lid, handed them to me, and placed the lid of the barrel on the stage floor. While I inspected the rope and handcuffs, Sanjay took his bowler hat in his hands and rolled his neck back and forth before returning the hat to his head.

"I'll take these two," I said, holding up the more menacing-looking pair of handcuffs and a piece of thick rope.

"Two," Sanjay murmured. "Very nice."

He turned away from me and placed his wrists together behind his back.

"Make them as tight as you'd like," he said.

So I did.

I wouldn't have thought a person could fit into the barrel, especially a man who was five foot ten with his hands tied behind his back, but Sanjay eased inside with little effort.

"If you'll place the lid securely on the barrel before returning to your seat," he said from within his confines.

As I secured the lid, I noticed the barrel rested on a footed stand that raised it several inches off the floor, so Sanjay wouldn't be able to go through a trap door in the stage.

For a few moments after I returned to my seat, nothing happened. Then the barrel began to rattle. Slowly, at first, for over a minute. As I began to wonder what on earth Sanjay was doing in there, the rattling grew more violent. Just as it was shaking so hard I was sure the lid would burst open, the movement ceased.

The stage was dead silent.

In the silence, a wisp of smoke escaped from the lid of the barrel, followed by a burst of yellow flames through a single hole cut out of the barrel. That couldn't be right.

"Sanjay?"

Silence.

"Sanjay, are you all right?"

More silence.

The flames grew brighter.

"Ewan!" I yelled. "Is this supposed to happen?"

"He's an expert," he called back from below the stage. "I'm sure he'll escape in time." He paused. "Uh…pretty sure."

"You mean he's still in there?"

With my heart thudding in my chest, I jumped onto the stage and ran toward the flaming whisky barrel.

TWO

As I ran toward the flaming barrel, the doors of the cabinet flew open. A hand reached out and grabbed my wrist, its fingers digging into my flesh.

Sanjay whirled me around, stopping me before I reached the fire. We watched from a few yards away as the flames exploded through the top of the whisky barrel. The planks fell flat, revealing only emptiness. The fire was gone.

"How could you not be inside there?" I asked, shaking free of Sanjay's grip. "I saw the space between the barrel and the stage. There's no way for you to have gotten out."

"A magician never reveals his secrets," Sanjay said. A look of self-satisfaction spread across his face.

"You didn't do that escape in your show at home." I felt my voice shaking as I spoke. I'd been so sure he was burning alive inside that barrel, and he was happy about it. Men.

"It's new," Sanjay said. "I thought a whisky barrel would be a good escape for a performance in Scotland. I've performed in England before, but not here."

"That wasn't funny," I grumbled.

"It's Ewan's fault!" Sanjay insisted. "He knew I wasn't still inside. It's supposed to be even more dramatic, with the effect drawn out. Just like Houdini did. But I had to cut it short since you ran onto the stage. What were you planning to do? Throw yourself on the flames?"

I glared at Sanjay. He took a step back.

"You could have told me what you were doing," I said. My voice was close to a growl.

"I had to make sure you wouldn't know what was supposed to happen," he said, his eyes pleading. "That's the whole point of having you watch, to see if you saw what you weren't supposed to see. I know you like to throw yourself into things, but I didn't think you'd do it so literally here."

"You were right," I said. "I shouldn't have volunteered to help. This is supposed to be a *relaxing* vacation."

"Why don't you throw yourself into having a relaxing day today. Do some sightseeing and I'll meet up with you later before my show."

"I have other things on my mind."

"Right." Sanjay pursed his lips and a dark expression came over his face. "What with you getting over that breakup and all."

I hadn't actually been thinking about my breakup. *Thanks, Sanjay.* I'd been thinking about whether I had time to buy myself some new clothes before meeting Daniella for the picnic lunch she was having to celebrate the start of her festival show, *Fool's Gold.*

Sanjay shook his head. "Anyway," he said, "the flames in this illusion weren't strong. But it was still very sweet of you to try to save me."

I know I should have left the theater right then, but curiosity about Sanjay's illusion made me decide to watch the trick again. Just one more time.

After I watched Sanjay escape from the empty whisky barrel a fourth time, I still hadn't figured out how it was done.

Each time, Sanjay took the whisky barrel backstage and reconstructed it within minutes, which gave me my first—and only—clue to the illusion. It had been specially constructed to come apart and reassemble easily, and to withstand flames without catching fire. It didn't tell me much. Only that Sanjay was a cruel friend for refusing to tell me how it was done.

The second member of Sanjay's crew arrived as Sanjay stepped out of the cabinet a fourth time and took a bow with his bowler hat in one hand and opened handcuffs and two pieces of rope in his other hand—one of the many variations I'd tried. Though I was tempted to stay even longer, I'd already stuck around longer than I intended. Glancing at the clock on my phone, I knew I was going to be unfashionably late to meet Daniella.

I replayed Sanjay's act in my mind as I left the theater. I had yet to figure out a single one of Sanjay's illusions. Even once I knew that Sanjay would materialize in the cabinet on the other side of the stage after squeezing himself into the whisky barrel with his wrists bound, I had no idea how he pulled off the switch.

I paused outside the theater to listen to a new voicemail message and give my eyes a moment to adjust. Dark storm clouds hung low in the distance, but the sun shone brightly above me. It had been darker in the theater than I'd realized.

Perhaps that was related to how Sanjay had pulled off his illusion....

My focus shifted when I heard the contents of the voicemail.

"I'm so sorry, Jaya." It was Daniella. "Late to my own party...a problem has come up...I'll be there as soon as I—" The message cut off abruptly.

I frowned at the phone. It wasn't the words she'd spoken that worried me. If anything, it was a relief to hear I had a little extra time. But I didn't feel relieved. Daniella's voice was shaking.

This was a woman who regularly performed on stage in front of hundreds, even thousands, of people. I'd never seen her nervous, and never heard her voice tremble like that.

Daniella Stuart had been an actress for years, and this Fringe Festival show was the first play she'd also written. She moved from her native Edinburgh to London to be an actress when she was a teenager, and had become moderately successful on the London stage. But after celebrating her fortieth birthday, Daniella wanted more. I met her the previous year at the British Library, where I was doing research on the British East India Company to finish my dissertation. She was at the library researching historical chess pieces for the two-person play she was writing. Even though she was over a decade older than I was, her carefree spirit made her a welcome break from my research in the library's reading rooms.

Whatever was making her that worried, it wasn't good.

THREE

I replayed the voicemail message. The only new thing I noticed was that she gave a slight, nervous laugh after saying she'd be late to her own party. What was going on?

Daniella's play, *Fool's Gold*, was scheduled to begin the following night, so today's picnic was a party her friends were throwing for her. It would have been a dinner except there was a big festival gala happening that evening she planned to attend.

I tried to shake off the bad feeling creeping up the back of my neck. It was probably nothing. I was jetlagged, starving, and dressed like a neon sign. Needless to say, I wasn't at my best. There must have been an innocent explanation. Daniella probably felt bad that I'd flown in from San Francisco and she was running late. Surely that was all there was to it.

I tucked my phone back into my messenger bag and hurried down a street lined with colorful shops at street level and faded stone facades above. The broad sidewalks were full of people watching street performers in town for the festival. I eased my way past a band of fiddlers surrounded by an enthusiastically clapping crowd, and around a teenage comedian who was making small children laugh as he pulled out colorful silk scarves from behind their ears. The energy of the crowd was contagious, and I found myself pushing my worries aside and smiling along with the kids.

The Edinburgh Fringe Festival was an eclectic combination of performances. It had grown into the largest performing arts festival in the world because they didn't keep anyone out. There were no applications. No juries to approve performances. Actors, comedians, dancers, musical theater troupes, and other performance artists needed to find financing to put on their shows, but there were shoestring budget street performances next to expensive productions. There was room for everyone.

Since Daniella was running late, I had time to stop by my hotel to take a quick shower. I said a silent thanks when I found my laundered clothes waiting for me. I wouldn't have to look like a florescent pink fashion victim when meeting up with Daniella and her friends.

After taking a three-minute shower, I changed clothes and towel-dried my hair while on hold with the airline. A harried call center employee regretfully informed me they had no idea where my bag was. *Great.* My jeans and sweater would do fine for today—as long as the looming storm held off—but my high heels wouldn't do for the scenic jogging routes or hiking I'd planned. I eyed the stranger's suitcase that looked so much like my own. I never imagined anyone besides me would have a vintage Wedgwood suitcase in blue with white trim. It was one of the things my dad had saved from is childhood in the 1950s, and I'd found it in the back of a closet at his house when I moved out of the house at age sixteen. I made a mental note to never again fail to pack an extra set of clothes in my carry-on bag.

I would also never again pack anything important in a checked bag. Earlier that summer I'd found a faded old letter about a chess game tucked into the pages of a book at a used bookstore in San Francisco, and I packed it to show Daniella, thinking she'd get a kick out of it. I wouldn't be arriving at the picnic with a fun conversation piece.

The hotel wasn't far from the Princes Street Gardens, where the picnic was taking place. As I entered the gardens, Edinburgh Castle loomed above me, the dark stone enclosure sitting on a mound of volcanic rock high above the center of the city.

The gardens were crowded with people attending the festival, but I was able to find Daniella's group thanks to a bright yellow poster board with hand-drawn black lettering that spelled out *Fool's Gold*. Two women sat on a picnic blanket next to the sign. In spite of the crisp wind, they were both dressed as if it was summer in southern California. They were drinking from plastic champagne flutes and speaking animatedly with each other in thick Scottish accents. Though it had taken me almost half an hour to arrive after receiving the voicemail message, there was no sign of Daniella.

As I walked up to the two women, they fell silent. They stared at me, wide-eyed. I was no longer wearing the bright pink gift-shop attire, so I wasn't sure what was so shocking about my appearance. I smoothed my hair, making sure I hadn't accidentally left a comb sticking out of it or some other silly thing I might have done in my sleep-deprived state. When I reached them, I realized it wasn't me they were staring at.

A middle-aged man came up from behind and stopped next to me. Now this was someone with an unforgettable appearance. He was dressed as if he was living in another era. He wore a perfectly tailored tweed jacket, glasses with thick gold-colored frames, a bright green ascot around his neck, riding boots over jodhpurs, and to top it all off: a deer stalker hat over his salt-and-pepper hair, a la Sherlock Holmes.

"This is Daniella's party?" he said in a posh English accent.

The two women murmured in unison that it was, scrambling to stand up.

"I hope I'm not intruding," he added.

"Not at all," the taller woman said. "It's great to have you. Daniella should be here soon."

"Champagne?" the second woman offered, swinging a bottle in one hand and lifting a platter of cheese and sliced baguette in the other. "Or Brie?" The open bottle swayed in her hand precariously. Clearly she'd had too much champagne and not enough cheese.

"I'd love some cheese," I said. The woman holding the cheese platter looked at me as if seeing me for the first time.

"Sorry!" she said. "You must be Daniella's American friend. She mentioned you were coming."

The women introduced themselves, but I immediately forgot their names. Between worrying about Daniella and wondering about the man in the outrageous outfit, I was far too distracted for multitasking.

"American, eh?" Sherlock said to me with an overstated wink as he accepted the glass from Daniella's eager friend.

"Guilty," I mumbled through a mouthful of bread and cheese. Travel had left me famished.

"Clayton Barnes," he said, extending his hand.

"Jaya Jones."

Clayton Barnes had one of the most enthusiastic hand-shakes I'd ever encountered. If his over-the-top attire and handshake were indicators, he was having a lot of fun with life.

The women smiled at him and told him to help himself to anything before giggling and sitting back down on the pic-nic blanket. They must have been pretty drunk to be giggling so much.

"Here for the festival?" Clayton asked me.

"Daniella and another friend of mine are performing."

"Have you attended before?"

I shook my head as I chewed and wondered if he was consciously trying to look like Sherlock Holmes. *Of course! The festival.* He was in costume.

"You're in for a treat," he said. "I've lived here for over ten years, and come to the festival each summer. But this one is special."

"That's why you're dressed up."

He looked at me blankly for a second while I froze, a sinking feeling in my stomach. I might as well have taken off my shoe and stuck my foot in my mouth along with the cheese.

But a moment later he broke into a large grin. "You mean my clothing for a midday picnic," he said with a smile. "I'm a bit old fashioned, I know. It's because of my avoca-tion. You see, I'm an alchemist—"

"An *alchemist?*" I interrupted.

"Yes." Clayton beamed at me, rocking back and forth in his riding boots. "An alchemist."

"You mean you study the history of alchemy?" I asked, holding out hope.

"Oh, no. I'm a practicing alchemist." He took a small sip from his glass, the cheap plastic looking entirely out of place in his hand. "Changing base metals into gold. It's how I made my fortune, you see."

Great. Daniella was late to her own party, possibly because something was horribly wrong, and I was stuck talking to the crazy guy who thought he was in a comic book.

"Uh huh," I said. I glanced over at Daniella's friends, wondering if I could join their conversation on the blanket.

"It's not as glamorous as it sounds," Clayton said. "It took over a decade of rigorous study before I was able to perfect the process. Now I'm connected to the elements to such a degree that I can sense the presence of gold. That's why I was intrigued by Daniella's show and why this year's festival is special. There's a gold and silver chess set—"

"The centerpiece of her show," I said. I'd heard about the idea from Daniella. Antiques dealer Feisal Khattabi was sponsoring Daniella's play at the festival, including the loan of an antique chess set made of gold and silver to be used in the show. It was a replica of the famous Lewis Chessmen. Feisal's gold and silver chess set had been commissioned by an eccentric Scottish laird who'd lost his bid to purchase the original Lewis Chessmen after they were unearthed in a remote region of Scotland in the 1800s.

"It's brilliant," Clayton said.

"I still don't understand the logic of using this chess set to drum up business for an antiques store," I said. "Doesn't the risk outweigh whatever buzz it might create?"

"Hardly," Clayton said. "Feisal has precautions in place. You said you haven't been to the festival before. There are tens of thousands of people here. Performers need to do something to stand out from the crowd. This chess set is great publicity for Feisal's antique business as well as Daniella's play. Here in Scotland, the Lewis Chessmen are a big deal. This gold and silver replica is almost as old—and perhaps even more valuable."

I held my tongue. It still sounded like a terrible idea. Whatever precautions might be in place, flaunting a valuable set in front of thousands of theatergoers sounded like very bad news.

"Do you know the history of the Lewis Chessmen?" he asked, reading my expression.

"I've heard of them," I said, "but don't know much about them. Aren't they in a collection at the British Library in London?"

"Don't remind the Scots," Clayton said with a wink. "Yes, that's them. Some of the pieces are in England, but many of the best pieces from the set are here in Edinburgh, and Scotland wants to get the rest back from England. There's a great deal of national pride wrapped up in those pieces. A farmer and his cow discovered the walrus-ivory and whale-tooth carved pieces on his land on the Isle of Lewis in 1831—which is why they're called the Lewis Chessmen. Nobody can agree on where they originally came from, but they are truly works of art."

"Aren't they supposed to be humorous in some way?" I asked.

"You know more than you said." Clayton gave me a mischievous grin.

"It's the curse of a historian," I said. "Whenever I know only a little bit of history about something, it's impossible to think I actually know anything about it."

"That humor you mentioned is one of the reasons the set has fascinated people since their discovery. Aside from the pawns, all the pieces are human figures, and real characters. The artists who carved the pieces created humanity that resonates across time and culture. A scowling king, a shocked queen, a crazed berserker rook. This gold and silver replica doesn't capture the details of the original, but you can see why it's still something that would interest a lot of people."

"All right," I said. "Maybe it doesn't sound like a *terrible* idea. But it's still a stressful idea. I wouldn't want to be the security guard in charge of safekeeping."

Clayton laughed heartily, but I didn't join in. I couldn't shake the memory of the usually confident Daniella's shaking voice on the phone.

"I wonder what's keeping Daniella," I said.

"And Feisal," Clayton said, his smile disappearing. "He wouldn't miss this celebration, either."

I breathed a sigh of relief as I looked past Clayton.

"Here she is," I said, pointing at two approaching figures.

Daniella was with a tall, waif-like blond woman who must have been the other actress in *Fool's Gold*. She gave us all quick hugs and introduced Astrid, all the while with a forced smile. Daniella's short brown hair had always been a bit unruly, but in a stylish punky sort of way. Today it was lifeless and messy, and her face creased with worry.

"Sorry Astrid and I are late," she said. "There was a security problem at the theater."

The sirens of police cars drowned out our voices as they passed us and sped down Princes Street. My eyes followed the cars. They screeched to a halt a block past us.

"What kind of problem were you talking about?" Clayton asked. "Not the chess set, I hope."

"A broken window," Daniella said. "They think it was a drunken prank. The city is crazy right now. But...."

"But what?" Clayton asked, adjusting his Sherlock hat. "As you said, it's festival time."

"It worried Feisal," Daniella said. "And I didn't like the look of it either. He wanted to make sure the theater got it fixed right away."

"Why did Feisal go?" Clayton asked. "That should be security's job."

Astrid gave an un-lady-like snort, detracting from her stunning appearance. She stood six feet tall in ballet flats, a full foot taller than me, though her bone structure was as small as mine.

Daniella wasn't looking at either Clayton or Astrid. Her gaze was focused past all of us.

"The police cars," she said. "That's our hotel."

She was right. The police cars had stopped directly in front of the Old Town Hotel.

Without giving us a backward glance, Daniella marched away from the picnic, heading straight for the hotel. Clayton squinted at Daniella through his gold-rimmed glasses, his expression unreadable. Astrid's face was set in an angry glare. Nobody made a move to follow Daniella except for me. I hurried to catch up with her.

"What's going on?" I asked when I caught up to her. She had her phone to her ear, but hung up when she saw me.

"I've had a bad feeling ever since this morning," she said, not slowing her pace. "It's always a bad sign for a show when something is sabotaged at the theater."

"What does that have to do with the hotel?" I asked. I was half-jogging to keep up with her. Not an easy feat while walking through a grassy park in heels.

"Maybe nothing," she said. "I hope it's nothing."

Daniella's friends hadn't followed, but Astrid and Clayton caught up with us at the edge of the gardens. The four of us entered the hotel together. We didn't get far. The elevator and stairway off the hotel lobby were blocked off with police tape, leaving the adjacent bar packed with wall-to-wall people. Families had squished themselves into the three tartan-patterned loveseats off to one side, and a lucky few were sitting in the half-a-dozen matching chairs. Everyone else stood wherever there was a free few inches of floor space. The crowd quickly swallowed us up, and I found myself separated from Daniella, Astrid, and Clayton.

I caught a glimpse of Daniella pushing her way through the crowd to the closest police officer. Before reaching him, she paused and changed course. She'd spotted someone.

A tall man with dark, olive-hued skin stepped through the main doors of the hotel lobby. He was easy to spot. The man had presence. This was the type of person you could easily imagine commanding the attention of the room. He wore a dark gray suit that must have cost several thousand dollars. In spite of his businessman's attire, he reminded me of an older version of someone I knew....

Daniella greeted him with a hug. I couldn't hear what they were saying to each other, but their animated body language made it apparent something was wrong. A group of exceptionally tall men with German accents walked past me, and I lost sight of Daniella. This was one of those times when I really hated being short.

Craning my neck, I spotted a deerstalker hat. Clayton Barnes. I made my way in that direction. When I reached him, he was with Astrid and Daniella. The charismatic man wasn't with them.

"It's the chess set," Daniella said, her voice shaking even more than it had on the phone. "A thief used explosives to blow up a safe in the hotel. The chess set has been stolen."

FOUR

"You can't be serious," Clayton said. He shook his head from side to side repeatedly, as if willing his words to be true. His previous calm disposition was nowhere to be seen, replaced by the demeanor of a small child throwing a tantrum. "How could this have happened?

"I don't understand how it happened," Daniella said, looking at the floor as she spoke. "It shouldn't have been possible."

"What do you mean?" I asked.

"We thought we were being so clever," Daniella said, her voice almost a whisper. Her lip quivered and her eyes filled up, but she kept the tears at bay. "We made a show of putting the chess set in the main safe at the hotel desk. But it was a fake set we gave them. Nobody was supposed to know the real chess set was in the safe in our suite."

"How did you learn what happened?" I asked. "Was it from the man I saw you talking with?"

"That was Feisal," Daniella said, nodding and meeting my gaze. "The chess set is his, so the police told him what about the theft. He's gone off to the police station with them."

So that was the antiques dealer, Feisal. He reminded me very much of a great uncle of mine I only knew from family photographs. Their faces were superficially similar based on skin color and the shape of their eyes, but my great-great uncle's photographs had captured a bold look in his eyes and in the way he carried himself. I recognized that same adventurous spirit in Feisal.

"I never trusted that security guard of his," Astrid said. Though she didn't seem to speak much, her voice was confident, verging on arrogant. Her accent wasn't Scottish or English, but I couldn't place it.

"You don't mean Izzy," Daniella said.

"Of course I mean Izzy," Astrid said. I placed the accent. Her English accent was tinted with French. "Who else would I mean? You said it yourself—since it was stolen from our suite, where the four of us were staying, it had to have been one of us. You, me, Feisal, or Izzy."

Clayton remained silent, looking between Astrid and Daniella with his deerstalker hat pulled low on his brow. He wore an expression that combined anger and confusion.

"He wouldn't—" Daniella began, but stopped short when she saw Astrid's expression.

"Well, you and I didn't do it," Astrid said, "and why would Feisal steal his own chess set? I'm telling you, it was Izzy—"

"May I have your attention, everyone!" A fair-haired man in a policeman's uniform stood on a chair near the reception desk to address the crowd with a thick Scottish accent. The din of the crowd lessened slightly, but didn't cease, which was probably because the policeman looked all of twenty years old. As someone who was often mistaken for an undergraduate while I was finishing my PhD, I should be more forgiving of people who look young but need to exert their authority. In two weeks, I'd be teaching undergraduates as an Assistant Professor of History. I'm twenty-nine, but I'm only five feet tall and have the same small bone structure as my Indian mom. I'm a good teacher and know my stuff, so I hoped I'd be perceived by my students as having more authority than this poor policeman.

"The other floors of the hotel will be opened up soon enough," the young officer said, raising his voice to be heard above the chatter. "But not immediately. Please go about your business and you should have access to your rooms again within an hour or two."

The crowd gave a collective groan. The police officer looked in our direction, then jumped down from the chair and walked straight to us. When he reached us, he glanced at the cell phone in his hand. On the screen was an image of the *Fool's Gold* poster with a picture of the two actresses.

"Daniella Stuart and Astrid Moreau?" he asked.

He asked Daniella and Astrid to go to the station for a few questions, since they were staying in the suite with the theft. In spite of the respectful manner in which the request was made, it didn't seem like a voluntary request.

"Of course," Daniella said. "Jaya, I'll meet you back here as soon as we're done."

Instead of finding out why a security guard of questionable character was guarding the chess set, I watched Daniella and Astrid disappear out the door.

Clayton removed his gold glasses and rubbed his eyes. "I hope their input can shed some light on this mess," he said. "God, this is awful. Join me for a pint while we wait?"

I didn't want a beer, but my stomach rumbled loudly. Clayton and I made our way through the lobby toward the hotel's restaurant. At least that's what we tried to do. It was entirely possible I would be crushed to death weaving my way through the crowded lobby. But the policeman's words were beginning to have an effect on the hotel guests. The crowd thinned out and I spotted two seats at the end of the bar.

I passed a woman speaking with her young son, who fell silent and turned to stare open-mouthed at Clayton as we passed. It wasn't just the woman. Several people turned their heads to stare at him as we walked by. Though his outfit was outrageous, the rude behavior surprised me.

I kept on walking until I reached the empty seats. I sat on a high-backed wooden stool and set my messenger bag at my feet. I expected Clayton would remove his Sherlock hat when we sat down, but he left it on.

"I knew Feisal's trusting nature would get him into trouble one of these days," Clayton said. His shoulders slumped as he rested his elbows on the bar.

"You think Feisal's security guard stole the chess set?" I asked.

"I fear so," Clayton said. "I've known Feisal for years. I've bought many antiques from his London shop, and he's become a good friend over the years. He was born in Egypt, educated in London. He fell in love with our great country and has been here ever since. He's a good man, but he lets his emotions get the better of him when it comes to business decisions—such as who he hires."

We ordered food from the bartender and I asked for a coffee to go with my leg of lamb since it was a bit early in the day for a beer. But as soon as the bartender set down a cup of instant Nescafé front of me, Clayton's dark beer looked much more appealing. I should have known better than to order coffee in a Scottish bar.

"I may drink far too many of these," Clayton said as he raised his glass, "unless the gold pieces are recovered soon."

"The police must know something they aren't sharing," I said. "Otherwise they would have questioned all the guests, not just the four of them staying in the suite."

"I suspect they will be arresting Izzy, if they haven't already."

"Why are you and Astrid so sure he's guilty?" I asked. "Shouldn't a security guard be the least likely person to be suspected?"

"It's his past," Clayton said. I waited for him to go on, but he didn't.

"Which is?" I asked.

"I don't like to gossip about others," Clayton said, drawing his lips together and adjusting his glasses. "It creates a negative energy that isn't good for my alchemical transformations. You needn't concern yourself with our problems. You're here to enjoy the festival. So tell me, what do you do in America?"

I opened my mouth to protest, but thought better of it. I couldn't figure out Clayton Barnes. He seemed sincere in what he was saying and oblivious to the stares brought by his flamboyant Victorian clothing.

He also had a good point. There wasn't anything I could do. I was only being nosy. I would wait for Daniella to return from the police station, since I said I'd wait for her, but then I would go buy myself some clothes and enjoy the city. There was a tour of the castle scheduled in a couple of hours that I had been hoping to attend. I love guided tours because it's interesting to see which parts of history the guides talk about.

"I'm about to begin teaching history at a university in San Francisco," I said.

"Oh, a historian! How lovely. That's why you asked if I studied historic alchemists. You don't study them, do you?"

"I specialize in Indian history," I said. "My research is on the British East India Company."

Clayton squinted at me through his glasses. "Are you Indian?"

"My mom was Indian and I was born there. But after she died, my brother and I grew up in California with my dad, who's American with typical mixed European descent."

"There were some extraordinary Indian alchemists," Clayton said. "Arguably the Egyptians did the most to further the study of alchemy, but there's a great tradition of Indian alchemy going back centuries."

"Really?"

"The Bhairavis focus on mercury, not gold, with the goal of prolonging life rather than transforming metals, but the processes are the same."

"Turning lead into gold is the same as the secret to eternal life?"

"They're both about transformation," Clayton said. "There's real science behind these transformations. Modern chemistry is but a branch of alchemy. Isaac Newton was an alchemist. He believed his alchemical work to be integral to his scientific studies. Aristotle was an alchemist, as was Socrates."

"You *are* a historian," I said.

"You caught me." He paused and loosened his ascot. "One needs to study the masters in order to learn their secrets."

"Let me ask you this," I said. "Why doesn't everyone go around turning lead into gold, if it's possible? And why don't we all live forever?"

Clayton frowned. "You're a skeptic. I understand. Most people are. They say I'm eccentric, that I have a screw loose. No, no. It's true. I know what they say. It's only natural. Most people cannot achieve the highest forms of alchemy, so it's perfectly reasonable that they doubt what they cannot see for themselves."

"Couldn't you show them?" I asked, thinking about Sanjay's tricks.

"It's not easy to transform metals," Clayton said. "Nor is it easy to transform oneself. And it's not something that can be done in public."

"Since you're one of the few people who have succeeded in this difficult process," I said, "why don't you make enough gold to solve all of the world's problems?"

"As a historian, surely you realize that money won't solve the world's problems."

"True enough," I admitted. "But it could help."

"And I do," Clayton said, a huge grin forming on his face. "You're not from here, so you don't know who I am. You see, I'm quite well known. I give a lot to charity."

I felt my cheeks flush. That explained why so many people in the crowd had been glancing in our direction. I was with a famous philanthropist.

It wasn't the Scottish people who were crazy. It was me who was ignorant. I'd been so caught up in my dissertation the last few years that even when living in London I hadn't heard of him. I hadn't had a television in my flat, and all of my reading was related to my research.

"I'm sorry I didn't realize—"

"Don't be embarrassed," Clayton said. "That's one of the reasons it's been such a pleasure to speak with you. I've spoken more to you about alchemy this afternoon than I've done with anyone in ages, because you haven't treated me condescendingly." He paused and reached into his breast pocket. "I'm hosting a little party for charity at my castle to-night, since so many people are in town for the festival. The process to create gold is draining, so I do what I can, and do-nate much of it, but I need to convince others to do so as well. I hope you'll attend—no donation expected, of course. You saw how upset Daniella is. You should help her take her mind off of this theft."

The elegant invitation he placed in my hand was print-ed on thick cream-colored paper with lettering that looked like gold leaf. Behind the letterpress text with information about the event was a light sketch of a stone castle surround-ed by a forest.

"I'm supposed to attend the opening night of my friend's magic show tonight," I said, "but if the timing works, I'd love to come. Thank you."

Clayton pursed his lips. I expected he wasn't used to people turning down invitations to his castle.

"I think you would be a big help to Daniella," he said. "You can distract her from this nonsense. The castle is just outside the city, so it takes no time at all to get there."

He tossed off the word "castle" as casually as if he was saying "apartment."

"It's only a small castle," he said, reading my expression. "No real fortifications. It's a glorified manor house with some beautiful gardens. It was owned by a sixteenth century alchemist. That's why I bought it. He's the one who named it Black Dragon Castle."

"Black Dragon?"

"It's an alchemical term," Clayton said. "It symbolizes stages of transformation. The dragon is key to transformations. Integral," he paused, "but dangerous."

FIVE

We'd finished eating and I was halfway through a pint of strong post-lunch beer when a familiar face appeared.

Daniella scanned the bar before spotting us and rushing up to me. She squeezed my hands, looking into my eyes with desperation. Smudges of eyeliner and mascara dotted her cheeks. She looked as if she might burst into a second round of tears any second.

"Is everything all right?" I asked, realizing it was a stupid thing to say as soon as it came out of my mouth.

"Where's Feisal?" Clayton asked. "How did you get here first?"

"Everything is wrong," Daniella said. She wiped an errant tear off her cheek.

"The theft is awful," I said. "But it doesn't sound like anyone got hurt. And surely Feisal has insurance."

"That's the problem," Daniella said. "I think he spent the last of his reserves insuring this promotion. He's nearly broke. His business suffered when the economy tanked. This was his last attempt to get the business back on track. The police are still questioning him, that's why he's not here yet. They think he stole his own chess set as *insurance fraud*."

"Oh dear," Clayton said. "The police can't really believe Feisal would steal his own chess set, would they?"

"That's what they seem to think," Daniella said.

"Desperate times make people do desperate things," I said.

"I've known him for years," Daniella said. "He's involved in London's theater community. He acquires specialty set pieces for high budget shows."

"I don't believe it either," Clayton said. "Feisal would never do that. I wouldn't say the same of everyone he employs...." He let the unspoken accusation hang in the air.

"Izzy," Daniella said, "would not have done this."

"Well, *somebody* had to have done it," Clayton snapped. "Unless you think it could have vanished into thin air?" His fists were clenched so tightly his knuckles were white. "Sorry," he said a moment later. He looked up at the ceiling as he took two deep breaths. "So sorry. It's this situation. The gold.... I can't believe it's gone."

"This is the worst timing for getting it back," Daniella said. "The police have too much going on with so many people in town for the festival. There's an inexperienced officer assigned to the case. He wants to wrap things up quickly, and the insurance fraud angle is simple."

Clayton groaned.

"Don't police often start with the assumption that it's an inside job?" I said. "That doesn't mean they'll continue to believe it if that's not where the evidence takes them. It doesn't sound so strange that that's where they'd begin."

"That's not the weird part," Daniella said. She turned to Clayton. "You weren't wrong when you said the chess set vanished into thin air."

"What do you mean?" he asked.

"There were a dozen witnesses in the hallway," Daniella said. "A German tour group in town for the festival. After the safe was blown opened, nobody came out of the room through the hotel room door. The police found the door hadn't been forced either. That means it was one of our keys that was used. It's both an inside job and an impossible job. There's no way the thief could have gotten out of that room. It's *impossible*."

SIX

"It can't be impossible," I said.

"Obviously," Clayton said with a scoff. "Izzy had to have gotten out somehow."

"Don't," Daniella said. Her voice was soft but firm. "Just because of his past—"

"I warned Feisal not to hire him," Clayton cut in.

"What am I missing?" I asked.

Daniella and Clayton looked sharply at each other, ignoring me. They stared at each other for a few seconds before Daniella looked away. She tucked a lock of her messy hair behind her ear and stared at the floor.

"It doesn't matter what we think," Clayton said. "The police will discover his culpability."

"But he didn't do it!" Daniella cried. "And now they're looking into Feisal. I know he didn't do it either. From what they said to me when they questioned me, I could tell they were just about to arrest him."

"The police aren't going to arrest an innocent man," I said in a voice I hoped sounded much more confident than I felt.

"Feisal!" Clayton called out. "We're over here!"

From a distance, I would have guessed the charismatic Feisal, with his thick black hair and thin build, was a young man. As he joined us I realized he must have been in his fifties. His face was lined with worry, making him appear even older.

"Clayton," Feisal said, shaking his hand heartily as he joined us at the bar. "I'm so sorry I couldn't make it to the picnic."

"What's the matter with you?" Daniella said. "That's the least of your problems."

"Proper respect is of the utmost importance at all times," Feisal said. "That's what will see us through this. I'm Feisal Khattabi," he added, turning to me.

"Jaya Jones."

"Ah, yes, Daniella's friend," he said, shaking my hand. "You are perhaps part Egyptian? Your beautiful features suggest—"

"I was actually wondering if you were part Indian. You remind me very much of a great uncle of mine—"

"Have you all gone crazy?" Daniella cut in, nearly shouting. "You're exchanging pleasantries while the chess set is missing, you're possibly going to be thrown in jail, and my play is supposed to open tomorrow!"

"Perhaps we should order Daniella some tea to calm her nerves," Clayton suggested.

"Quite," Feisal agreed.

"I. Don't. Need. Tea!" Daniella cried.

"Yes," Clayton said. "I see your point. This bar is no place for proper tea. Now that you two are here, we can adjourn elsewhere." He raised a finger in an understated motion to catch the attention of the bartender.

I knew about the reserved English, but Daniella had a point. Their forced calm was making my nerves tingle.

"Feisal," I said. "From what Daniella said, I'm surprised to see you here so soon. It sounded like the police were focusing their attention on you."

"They questioned me," Feisal said, "but they had no evidence to hold me. They had a theory about insurance fraud, but they now see that cannot be the case."

"What do you mean?" Daniella asked.

Feisal held his head high and cleared his throat. "After the fees to set up this show and to pay Izzy…" He broke off and looked past us at the row of spirits behind the bar. "I didn't have sufficient assets to adequately insure the set."

"But you told me—" Daniella said.

"I didn't want you to worry, Daniella," Feisal said. "I needed you to feel comfortable acting with the chess set on stage with you. A big part of the publicity needed to be that your play was a marvelous show. I couldn't have you nervous about the chess set."

"Feisal," Clayton said, his voice clipped. "You know better than that."

Feisal pulled out a handkerchief from his pocket and wiped his brow. "Quite," he said. "The one time I neglect to get insurance…but never mind." He tucked the handkerchief back into this pocket with a shaky hand. "I'm sure the police will catch the thief and recover the set. Yes, we must have faith in the police. The theft seems impossible…but it can't be *impossible*, can it?"

"What are the police doing now?" I asked.

"Unfortunately," Feisal said, "I believe they're now focusing their attention on Izzy, because of his background."

"But that's all in the past," Daniella said.

"The police don't see it that way."

"It wasn't his fault," Daniella said. "It was a moment of weakness years ago. Everyone deserves a second chance."

"I don't believe he's guilty either," Feisal said. "I wouldn't have employed him as security if I felt different than you, Daniella. He's worked for me for years."

"I know," Daniella said. "You gave him a chance when nobody else would."

Feisal's eyes were downcast. "I only hope I'll be here to have a job for him once this mess is over. My father never wanted me to stay in this country. He wanted me to learn what I could here, but return home. Home. Such a strange word. Even if I lose my business, Britain is my home. If I lose the money from the chess set, I can rebuild my business. But if I am presumed guilty of this thing I didn't do…"

"You don't mean you could be deported?" I said.

"I'm a permanent resident," Feisal said. "But I don't know what would happen if I were to be found guilty of a crime."

"Don't worry," Clayton said. "We all know you didn't have anything to do with this. The police will see that. Shall we find that tea and leave police matters to the police?"

"I don't want to drink any tea!" Daniella said. Her distressed, bulging eyes reminded me of the rook chess piece who was biting his shield. The bartender gave her a sharp look.

"Feisal," Clayton said. "Even if the ladies don't want tea, how about you and I have a cuppa?"

Daniella and I followed the two men out of the bar. Clayton and Feisal left the hotel, a sea of heads turning in their wake. Daniella wanted to stay at the hotel to wait for Astrid and Izzy, so we found a spot in the corner of the lobby with a good view of the front doors.

"What am I going to do?" Daniella asked.

"Clayton is probably right that the police will get to the bottom of this," I said.

"You don't understand, Jaya. The police will be biased in this case. I wish I had Clayton's faith in them, but I don't."

"With what you told us about the crime," I said, "I might have an idea."

"You do?" She wiped a tear from her cheek.

"I know someone who might be able to help. He thinks...*differently* than the police."

"Differently?"

"He creates seemingly impossible situations for a living."

"Please, Jaya. Anything that could help, please do it."

I pulled my phone from my bag and sent a text message to Sanjay.

Sanjay pulled apart the impossible acts of other magicians all the time, and this theft reminded me of such an illusion. If Sanjay could figure out how the impossible was done, he could help prove it wasn't one of the people involved in the play who'd stolen the set. It looked like Daniella was close to a nervous breakdown about Izzy being persecuted. I couldn't enjoy a relaxing vacation when my friend was convinced an innocent man would go to jail.

Beyond Daniella's worries, an image of Feisal's frightened eyes stuck in my mind. I hated to think about him losing his business and being forced to leave the place he thought of as home.

I'm named Jaya Anand Jones after my great-great uncle Anand, the first of the Indian side of my family to come to the United States in the early 1900s. I'd heard countless heroic stories about him from my mom when I was a kid. Like Anand, Feisal had created a life for himself in a new country, and had been willing to take a chance on someone he believed in.

Daniella bit her lip. "Do you really think your friend will be able to help?" she asked.

"I'm not sure, but it's worth a try." A text message flashed on my screen. "He texted me back that he'll come over to the hotel as soon as he can."

"What do you think is taking Izzy and Astrid so long at the police station?" she asked.

"Astrid is right here," a female voice said.

"Oh, Astrid," Daniella said, giving her a hug and clinging to her for several seconds. "What's going on?"

Astrid gave a graceful shrug. I wouldn't have been surprised if she worked as a model in addition to being an actress.

"Izzy should be along shortly," Astrid said.

"They're not holding him?" Daniella asked.

"He couldn't have done it," Astrid said.

"Thank God the police came to their senses about this being an inside job," Daniella said.

"I didn't say that," Astrid said. "Come, let's go outside. I need a cigarette."

"How can they have cleared the four of us but still say it's an inside job?" Daniella asked as we left the lobby.

The sidewalk outside was even more crowded than the hotel, full of street performers and people in town for the festival, but it felt like a different world outside in the fresh air.

"Who said they cleared us?" Astrid said. "They told you the same thing, that we were to remain available? Yes, that means we are all still under suspicion. All of us except for Izzy."

"Can someone please tell me what on earth this Izzy did?" I asked.

Astrid tilted her head back to blow out a puff of smoke. "Of course Daniella wouldn't tell you," she said. "She's sweet on big old Izzy."

"Just because I think he deserves a second chance," Daniella said, "doesn't mean I have a thing for him." She blushed as she spoke the words.

"He used to be a policeman," Astrid said. "He was caught taking bribes."

"*One* bribe," Daniella snapped. "A weak moment, when his wife was dying of cancer and needed extra care."

Astrid rolled her eyes. "A lot of people agree with her," she said to me. "He hasn't had a problem finding private security gigs. Feisal loves him, and not just because he's such a big guy that he can either scare away or beat up anyone out to steal Feisal's antiques. Oh, and that big size of his?" she turned back to Daniella. "That's why he's off the hook."

"They found how the thief got out?" she asked.

"That's what they implied," Astrid said. "Didn't they ask you about how tall you were, Daniella?"

"They did," Daniella said, "but I didn't think anything of it."

"Well, I asked. They were trying to figure out which of us could have gotten out through the window. Izzy is the only one of us who is obviously too big to have gotten out that way."

"But the suite was five floors up."

Astrid shrugged. "There has to have been some way out. It's not as if it was magic."

SEVEN

In spite of the fact that Sanjay's show premiered that night, he left his theater to meet us outside the hotel.

"A locked room," Sanjay said after he greeted us, already wearing his tuxedo. "How could I resist?"

"That's all you care about?" Daniella said. "The puzzle? This is my life."

Sanjay frowned.

"Finally," Astrid said. "Someone who says what they really mean." She smiled seductively at Sanjay.

"Of course that's not all I care about," Sanjay said. He gave me a quick glance with wide eyes.

"Sanjay's magic show opens tonight," I said. "Shall we get down to business?"

"Which is what, exactly?" Daniella asked.

"Let's go over everything you two know," Sanjay said.

"What, you're like one of those fake psychic detectives on television?" Astrid asked. "You can pick out some minuscule detail the police missed?"

Sanjay's shoulders visibly tensed and his eyes narrowed.

"I make my living as an escape artist," he said slowly. "I have never failed in any escape I've attempted, and I have come up with challenges even Houdini never dreamed of. I can free myself from anything anyone can construct. You seem to have an impossible escape. Do you want my help or not?"

Sanjay isn't known for his modesty.

"We do," Daniella said quickly.

Astrid shrugged.

I went over the basics of who was involved with *Fool's Gold* and the chess set.

"None of us were here at the hotel when the theft took place," Daniella added, "so I'm not sure what more we can tell you."

"Where were you?" Sanjay asked.

"Astrid and I were together," Daniella said. "Jaya was there, too."

"I suppose the police have the hotel room roped off as a crime scene," Sanjay said. "Whose room is it?"

"It's a suite we're sharing," Daniella said. "Feisal and Izzy are sharing one of the bedrooms, and Astrid and I are in the second bedroom of the suite. I suppose we'll all need new rooms tonight." She paused and shook her head. "All these rooms have high-end safes in them, that's why Feisal selected this hotel. It was supposed to be the safest place to keep the chess set when we weren't using it on stage for a performance. We rehearsed with a regular chess set painted gold and silver."

"Who knew the chess set would be in the hotel room safe?" Sanjay asked.

"Only the four of us," Daniella said. "Me, Astrid, Feisal, and Izzy. That must be why the police think it was one of us."

Astrid gave a short laugh. "It wouldn't have been difficult to figure out, would it? Anyone who saw the advertisements about the famous chess set appearing in our show would have known the set had to be locked up somewhere. It's not like we're in disguise when we return to the hotel. We've been here for days. And we used our real names to register."

"That's not true," Daniella said. "I mean, it's true we've been here for days and used our real names, but nobody would have guessed the set was in the hotel room. Feisal made a big deal about pretending to give it to the hotel staff to put it in the hotel's bigger main safe. Anyone paying attention to us would have thought the set was in that safe, not the room safe."

"You mean there's a duplicate fake chess set in the hotel's safe?" Sanjay asked.

"Exactly." Daniella rubbed her eyes, smearing her eye makeup even more. "I'm making this worse, aren't I? Making it seem like it has to be one of us. Feisal gave the front desk a spray-painted fake set, just like the one we're using in our rehearsals. The set's in a box, so unless someone tried to steal it they wouldn't even get a close enough look to know it was fake."

"Interesting," Sanjay said. He placed his fingertips together in an overstated show of thoughtfulness, as if he were performing. "I need to get back to the theater to get ready for my show. Don't you want to walk me out, Jaya?"

"What are you talking about?" I said. "We're already outside."

"Don't be dense," Astrid said. "He wants to talk with you in private. We'll be inside." She stubbed out her cigarette.

"You gotta love the French," Sanjay said after they'd gone inside.

"What couldn't you say in front of them?" I asked. "They didn't steal the set. They have alibis. You heard them. They were together."

"Do you want my cape?" Sanjay asked, pulling a thin red cape from an inner pocket of his tuxedo jacket. "You look like you're freezing to death."

"I wouldn't say no to the jacket."

Sanjay hesitated.

"What?" I said. "You don't trust me with one of your custom magic act jackets?"

"It's not that I don't *trust* you...."

"Never mind," I said, ignoring the goose bumps I felt under my sweater. This was what passed as summertime in Scotland? "I'm fine."

"Anyway," Sanjay said, tucking the thin cape back into his pocket, "all their alibis prove is that they didn't act alone. They could be in on it together. But I tend to believe her. Not because of her alibi, which I'm sure the police will check out. Even if it checks out, they could have hired someone to steal the set for them."

"Someone who can disappear into thin air," I cut in.

"We'll get to that," Sanjay said. "Daniella seems genuinely upset. She's a wreck."

"She *is* an actress," I said. "But I don't think she's acting. Why would she ask for our help if she's guilty?"

"Agreed," Sanjay said.

"Why didn't you ask more questions?" I said. "I thought you were all about the details?"

"I am," Sanjay said. "But I can't get into that room right now, and I'm not the one who's going to be able to get any useful details from Daniella. You are. She trusts you. You should stay with her."

"She's going to a festival gala tonight."

"Can you go to with her?"

"I have an invitation, but I'm coming to your show to-night."

"I've got nine more performances after tonight," he said. "It's more important that you find out everything you can about what Daniella knows. She'll feel more comfortable with you, especially once she's out drinking."

"You're saying you want me to take my friend out to a gala at a castle and get her drunk."

"You've got a rough life, Jaya, but somebody has to do it."

EIGHT

Sanjay left and I went back inside. I maneuvered through the still-crowded lobby. A man with a shiny bald head was talking with Daniella and Astrid. I knew at once this was Izzy. He wasn't tall or fat, but the descriptions of the man had been correct. He was muscular, though not quite like a body builder. It looked like his natural frame was to be a big guy, which he'd supplemented with muscle. His shiny head had been shaved completely bald, and he looked to be a few years older than Daniella and Astrid.

"I didn't do this," he was saying to Daniella. He put an awkward hand on her shoulder, hesitating for a moment as if unsure if he should follow through and give her a hug. "I swear to you."

"I know," she said.

Izzy squeezed her shoulder, then dropped his arm. Daniella's face fell. She smiled a moment later when she saw me.

"This is Jaya," Daniella said, introducing me to Izzy. "A friend who's in town for my show. She's staying here at the same hotel. Thought we'd have more time to hang out together that way." She gave a bitter laugh. "I suppose that worked out, though not as I imagined."

Izzy gave me a vigorous handshake and looked at me squarely with bright blue eyes. "Good to meet you," he said.

"Why don't you tell her the truth, Izzy?" Astrid said. "That it's *not* nice to meet her, because you'd rather be anywhere but here."

I tried to stop myself from smiling. Astrid was brash, but she was right. All of these English guys were so proper they'd be sure to pop at some point if they didn't let out their frustrations.

"Leave it to you, Astrid," Izzy said, "to make a bad situation even more uncomfortable."

"I'm going back outside to have another cigarette," Astrid said. "The three of you can stand around exchanging fake pleasantries for the rest of the afternoon. Jaya, it's been real. Really awful."

As Astrid turned and walked out, several male heads turned and watched her.

"She's not normally like that," Daniella said once Astrid was gone. "It's the stress of what's happened."

"Yes, she is," Izzy said. He sighed, his large shoulders swaying close to Daniella. I could have sworn I saw her give him a longing glance, but it only lasted a second.

"Don't worry about me," I said.

I felt like a third wheel, but I knew I couldn't leave. Sanjay was right that I should stay with Daniella if I wanted to help her and Feisal. The two shy lovebirds could figure things out once the theft of the chess set was resolved.

Besides, I wasn't feeling especially generous when it came to other people's romances, since my own recent year-long relationship had ended only a couple months before. I wouldn't exactly say I was bitter. Well…Who was I kidding? I was bitter. This was the start of a new phase of my life. It wasn't being alone that bothered me; I'm used to being on my own. It wasn't even worrying about whether I could pull it off; I'm a damn good historian. No, what left me apprehensive was that *everything* in my life was new. A new home, a new career as a professor of history, the start of a new life.

"What did the police tell you, Izzy?" I asked, bringing myself back to the present.

"Not much. They were awfully keen on me at first, but then they found out something else that made them think I didn't do it."

"You mean the fact that you couldn't have gotten out through the window," I said.

"You two have already been going over this, then."

"It's all I can think about," Daniella said. "How can they think one of us did this?"

"There was no forced entry into the room," Izzy said.

"Surely that's a mistake." Daniella's voice grew agitated as she spoke.

"I suppose someone could have gotten in through the window, too," Izzy said. "A really tiny person." He glanced in my direction. "But it doesn't make sense. We were the only ones who knew the chess set was there in our suite."

"You remember how tiny those windows were," Daniella said. "See, it's got to be someone else. Maybe it was one of the acrobats from one of the other performances." Her face lit up at the idea.

Izzy's gaze lingered on Daniella's with fondness. "I wish it was," he said. "But there's no way around it. It was one of us."

NINE

I didn't have time to go shopping for a dress. I didn't think my jeans and black sweater, or my new leggings and florescent pink t-shirt, would be appropriate attire for a fund-raising gala for the arts.

It was less than thirty minutes before Daniella said we had to leave. Daniella hadn't been allowed back into her suite, but her luggage was cleared and returned to her, so she had moved into the room of a performer she knew with an extra bed in a different hotel. I hadn't thought about asking her to borrow a dress until she was already gone.

Twenty-five minutes.

I eyed the stranger's suitcase. It couldn't hurt to take a closer look inside. The woman who owned this vintage suitcase had taken good care of it, and she'd taken good care of the contents of the suitcase as well. At least ten carefully folded 1960s-style dresses lay before me. I didn't recognize any of the names on the labels, but these were stylish clothes. A polka-dot polyester dress, a gingham dress suit, a tennis outfit.... I could never pull off any of these.

But what about this one? I pulled out a gorgeous black dress with embroidered white details. It was a little big for me, but not too bad. It came with a dainty white belt that cinched the waist. This might just work.

I had black high heels with me. At my height, they're my standard shoes, so I'd worn these stilettos on the flight. I slipped into the dress and stepped into my shoes. I glanced at my scruffy messenger bag lying on the bed. It wouldn't do. The open suitcase lay next to my bag. A shiny white clutch made of vinyl was tucked into the side of the suitcase.

A knock sounded at my door.

"Jaya," Daniella's voice called through the door. "Clayton felt bad for us with the theft so he's sent a car to take us to the party. It's waiting."

No time to worry about taking the clutch. I grabbed it with my wallet and phone, and was out the door.

Downstairs, a gold Bentley waited to escort us to the castle. Astrid was already in the back when Daniella and I climbed inside the plush seats. She wore a strapless red dress that went down to her ankles with a slit that went up to her thigh. Her long blond hair fell over her bare shoulders with a hint of curl.

"Your dress is the wrong size," Astrid said to me.

"Long story," I said.

"Astrid is a model," Daniella said. Aside from redness of her eyes giving away she'd been crying, Daniella looked like she could have been a model that night as well. I'd never known her to dress up more formally than jeans and a t-shirt when she wasn't on stage, but tonight she wore a form-fitting silver dress with gold ankle boots. Her short brown hair was spiked stylishly.

"Used to be," Astrid corrected Daniella. "I used to be a model."

"Your outfit," I said to Daniella. "Publicity for your play?"

"Do you like it?" she asked.

Before I could answer, Astrid cut in, "Nobody will notice you're wearing gold and silver because of the play, because nobody cares about the play. There are too many performances at the festival. We should have stayed in London."

With that start to the evening, I was relieved the drive to Clayton's castle took only fifteen minutes. It took longer to drive from my apartment to my university in San Francisco. The castle was just outside of Edinburgh, right off the A7 freeway.

Edinburgh was a northern enough city that the sun was still high in the sky late into the evening, so for the whole drive I had a perfect view of my surroundings from the window of the luxurious back seat. As soon as the chauffer pulled off the freeway, all evidence of the twenty-first century disappeared. We were swallowed up by a grove of evergreen trees. A bright blue river ran along the side of the winding road. The car slowed as the road and river curved. In a clearing of trees, the turret of a castle overlooked the river.

The Bentley turned off the road and drove up a circular drive; the red stone castle came into full view. I relaxed a little. Though it was a castle, it was mansion-sized rather than football-stadium-sized. I gripped the white clutch in my hand and took a deep breath. I might not be able to handle a gala at a castle, but I could handle a party at a mansion.

I couldn't help shivering while I walked from the car to the castle. It wasn't my nerves. The fickle Scottish weather had turned the crisp breeze from earlier in the day into a full-blown arctic wind.

Champagne flowed freely as guests milled around the grand room of the castle. Tapestries filled with birds lined two walls. One tapestry featured a phoenix rising out of the flames, the other was a black dragon surrounded by flying pelicans and other winged creatures.

Two winding staircases led from the grand ballroom up to a balcony overlooking the party. In the balcony, a single framed painting stood on an easel. It was this painting that was being used to raise money that evening. A modern painter who critics were praising had painted a scene of Edinburgh Fringe Festival street performers. It was being given away as part of a charity raffle that evening. The cost to enter the raffle was £5,000 per ticket.

I spotted Clayton shortly after arriving. He wore a black tuxedo with gold-colored wingtips and a top hat made of gold cloth. When he saw me, he came over and asked if I was doing a good job forgetting about the theft and distracting Daniella from her anxiety about Izzy. I assured him his party was doing a good job helping us both forget our worries.

Astrid had been swept away by a balding man claiming to be a duke of some sort, and Daniella and I were talking with an elderly couple who'd heard about Daniella's play and were intrigued. Astrid's gloomy prediction hadn't come to pass. They weren't the first people who had come up to Daniella to ask about her show.

"The chess set in *Fool's Gold* is both literal and figurative," Daniella was telling them. "The play is set in the neighborhood I grew up in. The wrong side of the tracks, as my American friend Jaya here would say. The characters Catriona and Alexis were best friends as kids. Catriona's father taught her how to play chess when she was a little girl, before he was killed in an industrial accident. Catriona taught Alex how to play, and the two of them grew up with chess as their escape. Even though chess meant the most to Catriona, it was Alex who had the real aptitude for it. She's the one who was able to make it out of there. She got a scholarship to university, leaving Catriona behind. The title *Fool's Gold* is based on the chess term 'fool's mate,' and the gold represents both their friendship and a special chess set they use."

"That's nice, dear," the elderly woman said with a thick brogue. "But what about the *theft?*"

Daniella's face fell. News had leaked that the chess set had been stolen, which was turning out to be even better publicity than showing the gold and silver chess set at the Scottish festival in the first place. She smiled and told them the investigation was ongoing. but she hoped they'd enjoy the show.

"Doesn't anyone care about my play?" she said to me once they'd moved on, downing the last of her third champagne.

"If the news stories get them to come to your play," I said, "then who cares if that's the thing that gets them in the door?"

"Oh God," she said, picking up another champagne from a passing waiter. "What if the police think one of us did this for *publicity?*"

It wasn't a crazy idea. But I didn't have time to respond before Astrid joined us.

"He wasn't a real duke," Astrid said. "Can you believe it? He's only distantly related to one."

"What about that new guy you said you were seeing?" Daniella asked her.

"What guy?"

"You took a break from rehearsal yesterday morning to call him."

Astrid stared blankly at Daniella for a few seconds. "Oh yes," she said. "Him."

But it was a moment too late. She was lying.

TEN

"You forgot you were dating someone?" I asked Astrid.

"You were gushing about him yesterday," Daniella said, followed by a small hiccup.

"Are you two the good-girlfriend police?" Astrid said, her bright red lips set in a pout. "There's got to be some real royalty here somewhere. I'll leave two prudes to yourselves."

She stormed off, several men turning to watch her as she walked by.

"What's the matter with her?" Daniella asked.

"How well do you know her?" I asked.

"You think *Astrid* stole the chess set?" She shook her head. "But I was with her."

"She could have hired someone."

"She doesn't have that much imagination," Daniella said. "Oh God! That sounded awful, didn't it? Maybe I've had too many of these." She set her empty champagne class on a nearby side table. "No, I know Astrid can be difficult, but she's not a criminal."

Back at the hotel, I had to squeeze out the rest of the contents of the clutch to find the key to my room. How did women use these things? When I pushed open the door, my breath caught in my throat. The light of the room was on. I was certain I'd left it off.

"It's about time," Sanjay said.

"You were about this close to getting my knee in a very uncomfortable place." I flung my key at him. I wasn't surprised that he caught it. It disappeared from sight in the palm of his hand.

"You didn't leave me a choice." Sanjay placed the re-materialized key on the bed stand and sat down in the one chair in the small room. "You weren't answering your cell."

Sanjay was still wearing his tuxedo from his performance. His bow tie hung loose around his neck, and his bowler hat rested on the bed stand.

"My phone barely fit in this little clutch. I thought if I opened it I'd never get it shut again."

"You own a clutch? What happened to the messenger bag that goes everywhere with you?"

"It's not mine. I found it in the suitcase. I didn't think my messenger bag would fit in too well at the gala."

"You're stealing from this poor woman's suitcase?"

"*Borrowing*," I said. "Where do you think I got this dress? But I bet she's drinking the American whiskey I brought as a gift for Daniella and having the historical letter appraised."

Sanjay leaned back on his elbows and watched me.

"What?" I said, smoothing out the dress. "Do I have a big chunk of lint on me? God, please don't tell me I've got remnants of canapé stuck in my teeth."

"*You* were eating fancy food? Where's Jaya and what have you done with her?"

"Very funny."

Sanjay shook his head slowly but didn't say anything. "I was admiring your dress," he said finally. "You look…"

"Silly?" I said, slipping off my heels and flinging them into the corner of the small room. "I know. It's not really my style."

"That's not the word I was thinking of," Sanjay said. "Stunning is more like it. You look absolutely stunning."

"In this?" I looked down at the vintage black and white dress. "It's all wrong for my shape."

"Did anyone ever tell you that you don't know how to take a compliment?"

"It's hardly a fair assessment coming from a good friend."

Sanjay cleared his throat. "Why don't you dress like that more often?"

"I'm a professor, you know. Or at least I will be in two weeks. This dress doesn't exactly say "authority figure." I can't very well go around looking like a nightclub singer."

"I don't know. It has its charm. So who is this woman you stole it from?"

"Borrowed," I corrected him. "I have no idea. She didn't answer the phone number tucked into the suitcase. But she has great taste. The case was full of dresses like this. She's not as short as me, but she's thin, so this one worked pretty well since it has a belt."

I gave a little pirouette. Sanjay laughed.

"Sounds like your show went well," I said.

"Even better than expected. A woman fainted."

"Oh no!"

"No, that's a good thing," Sanjay said.

"It is?"

"Weren't you paying attention earlier?" he asked.

"Apparently not."

"You were supposed to be scared when the whisky barrel caught fire with me inside it. I cut short the effect when you were there, but with the fully drawn-out presentation, I was brilliant." He grinned as I rolled my eyes.

"What about that poor woman?" I asked.

"She's fine. She came to as soon as Ewan gave her smelling salts. The diversion allowed me to heighten the drama of the illusion."

"I'm sure she's traumatized."

"That's what people pay to see. If people didn't think I was truly putting my life at risk, I wouldn't sell out nearly as many shows as I do. Why do you think Houdini was so famous? He was a mediocre illusionist, but he understood the value of drama. Close-up magic baffled him, but give him the grand venue of an outdoor stage with a challenge to escape from a straitjacket while hanging upside down hundreds of feet above a crowd, and the public ate it up. But enough about my sell-out performances." He paused. "That's not why I'm here. How did the gala go?"

"No fainting was involved," I said, "but Daniella did get fall-down drunk. And even more interesting—Astrid is hiding something."

I sat down on the bed and tucked my legs under me. I went over the little I'd learned about the publicity for both the play and the chess set growing exponentially because of the press surrounding the theft, and I thought about Astrid lying about whatever she had to do away from the group the morning before the theft took place.

"Interesting," Sanjay said.

"That's it? That's all you're going to say? Aren't you going to say something about turning Astrid over to the police for the third degree?"

"That," Sanjay said, "would be jumping the gun." He pulled his cell phone from his pocket. After glancing briefly at the screen, he put it back and looked up at me. "It's late enough," he said.

"Late enough for what? I'm too wound up to sleep. My sneakers are in my missing suitcase so I haven't been able to go running, so I doubt I'll ever sleep again."

"That's not what I'm talking about. Let's go check out the room."

"You're not serious. The scene of the crime? I'm sure it's off limits."

"Of course I'm serious. How else are we going to solve this?"

"I'm sure the police have the room locked up."

Sanjay's forehead crinkled as he raised his eyebrows.

"Right," I said with a sigh. "The lock of that room won't be much different from this one."

"Exactly. You think I let myself into your room for kicks? The hotel is booked up, so I needed to practice on a door to a room I knew was empty."

"How long did it take you?"

Sanjay cleared his throat. "Let's not sit around discussing the details of how long it took to open what should have been a straightforward lock."

"Touchy, touchy."

"I've got jet lag." He yawned. "At least this hotel is proud enough of its historic roots that it still uses real old-fashioned keys. Those modern key cards aren't nearly as easy to break into with the set of skills I've got at my disposal."

"I'll remember that the next time I book a hotel room."

"Shall we?" Sanjay said.

I hesitated.

"You can either leave this to the police and see your friends go to jail," Sanjay said, "or we can take a look."

"I'm not going to talk you out of this, am I?"

"If you don't come with me, I'll do it on my own."

"Let me change," I said.

Sanjay's face fell. "Can't you go in that?"

"This is hardly cat burglar attire."

"Exactly. It's the perfect cover. If we're caught, our excuse is that we've just come from one of the festival's parties and we're drunk. That way we'll only get a drunk-and-disorderly warning—or whatever its British equivalent is—rather than being charged with what we're really up to."

I opened my mouth but Sanjay kept speaking.

"But we're not going to get caught," he said. "Especially with you as my lookout. Coming?"

I picked up the white clutch, slipped my heels back on, and followed Sanjay out the door.

"Three minutes, forty two seconds," Sanjay said.

I turned toward him from where I stood a few paces away in the hallway, holding my heels in my hand and trying to look tipsy to anyone who might see us skulking around the burgled room. Sanjay turned the handle and opened the door.

The room was completely dark. We locked the door behind us and Sanjay turned on the light.

"There's nothing more suspicious than flashlights," Sanjay said.

"You mean if we happened to have flashlights," I pointed out.

"Touché."

The suite wasn't much bigger than a standard hotel room in the US. The door opened into a small hallway. To the right, a bathroom that would have been at home in an airplane. To the left, two bedrooms that looked like they were previously one larger room. Straight ahead, a sitting room barely big enough to fit two chairs, a coffee table, and a loveseat in a tartan print matching the furniture in the lobby. The loveseat faced a television mounted on the wall, and next to the television was a hole where the wall safe had been. The wallpapered wall surrounding the safe was blackened, and the remnants of the safe's metal door hung askew.

In addition to the evidence of the explosion around the safe, the room showed other scars of the theft: the furniture was soaking wet. The sprinkler on the ceiling had done its job.

Neither the sitting room nor the bathroom had a window. That luxury was reserved for the two bedrooms on the opposite side of the hallway, each with one small window. Each bedroom had enough room for two twin-size beds— that looked smaller than standard twin-size to me—about two feet apart. The tall, narrow windows were in the space between the beds. Neither room had built-in closets, but instead had antique wooden wardrobes.

Sanjay ran his fingers along the edging of the floor-boards through the whole suite, then did the same thing along the walls. While he did two slow, meticulous circles, I studied the windows. They were small, almost like the openings for archers in a castle. There was no reason to have bigger windows for a view, since the windows faced another old building a few yards away. I looked around the edges of both windows. Typical of hotel windows, these windows didn't open. How had the police thought someone could have gotten out through one of them?

Sanjay came up behind me at the window and rested his chin on my head. I moved out of the way and let him examine the window.

"Nothing out of the ordinary here," he said. "Thick stone walls, solid construction."

"You thought there would be a secret passageway?"

"Not really. But one has to be thorough. Damn. This window doesn't open, either," he said, frowning. He pressed his forehead to the glass and looked down, and then up.

"Fifth floor," he mumbled to himself, staring out the window. "Sprinklers…no fire escape. Even if the thief could have altered one of these windows to open and get out, squeeze through the opening, and slide down a rope—or walk across one to the opposite building, if we want to entertain really outrageous ideas—there wouldn't have been time. They'd need to replace the window to its present state. No, the only way out of this place is that front door."

"Which a whole group of German tourists say didn't happen."

"Nobody got out through these windows," Sanjay said. "I don't like this at all, Jaya."

ELEVEN

Sanjay locked the suite behind us. We walked back to my hotel room in silence. I left Sanjay in the room while I used the bathroom to change.

"I've been thinking about the witnesses," Sanjay said when I emerged in my bright pink t-shirt and leggings.

"Unless this is an amazingly huge conspiracy we're stuck in the middle of, the tour group of Germans isn't lying."

"But what if they weren't lying," Sanjay said. "What if there was a way for the thief to get out of that suite through the door and have the witnesses think they never saw anyone come through the door?"

I eyed Sanjay skeptically. He was again seated in the desk chair, his elbows resting on his knees as he leaned forward and spoke earnestly.

"Don't you see?" he said. "A *diversion*."

"You mean like one of your stage tricks with smoke and mirrors."

"Something like that," he said. "Not smoke and mirrors literally, but an illusion of the same kind."

"You think they all looked away at a cute puppy at the same exact moment, right after an explosion sounded?"

"What if—" he leaned forward even farther. "What if the thief changed the room numbers?" He sat back and clasped his hands behind his head.

I thought about it for a minute. Could the thief have made a simple switch that made him invisible without being invisible?

"Brilliant, isn't it?" Sanjay said.

But it wasn't. Not in this case.

"You're forgetting something," I said. "The Germans didn't care about the room number—they heard the room the explosion came from. So unless this thief is a mastermind genius who has figured out how to move the sound of an explosion and the accompanying smoke from one floor to another, that explanation doesn't work."

Sanjay dropped his hands and grabbed his bowler hat. He ran his fingers along the rim like he always did when he was thinking.

"I don't like this," he said again.

"I don't either. This whole thing is a big mess for Daniella's play and Feisal's business."

"Not just that," Sanjay said. He stopped tracing the hat with his fingers. "This isn't a normal crime. I don't like that we don't know what we're dealing with—and that you're wrapped up in it."

"What do you mean? You think I'm in danger?" I hadn't stopped to consider the possibility. I don't think of myself as easily frightened, but a wave of mild panic came over me as Sanjay spoke in a more serious tone than I'd ever heard him use before.

"I shouldn't have asked you to investigate with Daniella and Astrid tonight," Sanjay said. "Since it seems like Astrid is somehow involved—"

"Weren't you listening?" I said, trying to convince myself as much as Sanjay. "Astrid was with Daniella during the theft."

"Your point being?"

"You know what my point is," I snapped. "That would mean Daniella is lying, too, and that she's involved. Then why would she ask for our help? We already went through this."

"I know," Sanjay said. "But we're missing something important. Maybe she wanted to throw suspicion off of herself."

"She already has an alibi of Astrid," I said. "Why would she risk us figuring out she was involved if she was already in the clear?"

"She could be a dupe," Sanjay said.

"Of Astrid, you mean? So what do you want to do?"

Sanjay and I stared dumbly at each other for a full minute, neither of us attempting to speak.

"Police?" I said.

"Police," Sanjay agreed.

"Now?"

"It's almost three o'clock in the morning."

"Good point." I yawned. "We can go in the morning. Meet me back here an hour before your show."

"Not enough time. But that doesn't matter. I'm sleeping here."

"*Excuse me?*"

"I'll sleep on the sofa. Until we know what's going on, I'd feel a lot better keeping you in my sight."

"I repeat: excuse me?"

"I said that badly. But you know what I mean."

"Do I? Why don't you enlighten me?"

Since I'm only five feet tall in thick socks, my dad made sure I could take care of myself. He drove me in his VW van all around the greater Berkeley area to every kind of martial arts class that existed. I stuck with jui-jitsu the longest, and I was fairly certain I could overpower Sanjay. I hate it when people underestimate me.

Sanjay swallowed hard. "I mean...you're handy to have around. If we get cornered, I can make myself disappear and you can arm wrestle the bad guy." He looked at me expectantly.

I smiled and gave him a kiss on the cheek. "I know that's not what you were going to say," I said, "but thank you. Together, I think we'll be fine. And sure, to save time, that makes the most sense for you to stay here. That's stupid for you to sleep on the tiny sofa, though. The bed is big enough for both of us."

"Uh..."

"What? You're like my brother, Sanjay. Why does it matter?"

"I'll be fine on the sofa," he snapped. He stepped into the bathroom and shut the door harder than was necessary.

What was the matter with him?

The next thing I remembered, something was tugging on my foot. I opened my eyes. It was Sanjay. He stood at the foot of the bed in his tuxedo trousers and a fitted white undershirt, his normally perfect thick black hair standing at all angles like

he'd been struck by a bold of lightning. I had assumed Sanjay's hair his fans swooned over was effortlessly perfect, but
clearly that wasn't the case.

"We overslept," he said. "I only have half an hour before I'm supposed to be at the theater. We're going to have to
go to the police after the show."

"Damn."

"Look, I'm going to catch a cab back to my hotel to
take a quick shower and grab a new tux—"

"You travel with multiple tuxedos?"

"Of course. At least six. Magic is dangerous business."
He winked at me, then turned serious again as he glanced at
the time on his phone. "Catch a cab to my show, okay?"

"But it's only a few blocks from here."

"Humor me," he said.

"Fine," I said. I had no intention of taking a cab for
what would be a five-minute walk, but Sanjay didn't need to
know that and worry for no reason.

Sanjay sighed. "All right. Don't take a cab. But be careful, okay?"

With that mind reading, he was out the door. Maybe
there really was some magic in the air. If there was, I definitely needed it. I didn't know what I was doing. This wasn't the
relaxing vacation I'd imagined.

On my walk to the theater I stopped at a take-out fish and
chips shop to grab some fried food to placate my growling
stomach. The cashier's accent was so thick that I'm not sure
what it was that I ordered, but the fried breading made up the
largest percentage of the meal wrapped in newspaper, and it

was delicious. The magic show was sold out by the time I got there, but the ticket taker had been left with a note from Sanjay to allow me backstage.

The lights flickered as I entered the theater, the sign that the show would begin shortly and everyone should take their seats. I didn't walk through the seats to get to backstage, so I couldn't see the crowd, but I could hear the overlapping excited voices with accents from across the world. I reached the dark backstage area near the stage as the curtain went up.

A solitary stage light illuminated the stage. Or rather, it illuminated a small part of the stage. Sanjay stood at the back of the stage in the shadows, his bowler hat resting on his head. He began to chant in a slow, rhythmic voice. He spoke in Punjabi, so I didn't understand what he was saying. But one didn't need to understand the words to feel what he was saying. As he spoke, one more light turned on, and a series of shadows flashed across the back of the stage. He was telling a story with simple cut-out figures that danced along the wall.

"Do you like it?" a soft voice asked in my ear.

Sanjay's voice. I think I jumped about a foot into the air.

"Jesus, Sanjay," I whispered back. "I thought you were on stage."

"What, that voice over? Do you like it? It's new." He straightened his bow tie. "That's just a shadow of me. A little more detailed than the projection of the stick figures, but pretty simple."

"That's not even another person up there?" My heart rate slowed closer to normal as I looked between the real Sanjay and the shadow on stage that I could have sworn was him.

"Nope. Just a projection. People see what they want to see. In this context, people assume it's me. The key to shows at the Fringe Festival is to keep things simple. Things are crazy enough putting on a complex show with bare bones staff. That's how I came up with this idea. The whisky barrel escape is the most complex of the illusions I'm doing here, but even that one is pretty simple—if you know the trick."

I gasped. It must have been a bit loud. Sanjay put his finger to his lips.

"Sanjay," I said. "I know how the thief did it."

"You do?"

"Sanjay," another voice whispered. I jumped again. I really hated how dark it was backstage. Ewan, the red-headed stagehand, came up beside us. "Cutting it close, aren't you?"

Sanjay swore. "Don't go anywhere," he said to me.

He turned and took the few steps to the edge of the stage. The stage lights shifted and the shadow I had assumed was Sanjay disappeared a fraction of a second before the real man stepped onto the stage. Applause sounded as I ran further backstage to think.

Just as Sanjay had led the audience to believe he was on that stage, the thief had done the same thing in that hotel room. Sanjay had been on the right track when he suggested a diversion that was an illusion.

The safe exploding was the illusion. By the time the explosion blew open the door of the safe, the chess set was already gone.

That meant the theft was no longer tied to an exact time we knew of. It could have been Astrid. But it could have been any of them. Our list of suspects with alibis was wrong. All wrong.

TWELVE

By the time Sanjay found me backstage in the green room after the show, I'd filled several pages of notepaper with thoughts about what was going on. Most of it was scratched out. My revelation meant we knew less than before.

"Not cool," Sanjay said, closing the door behind us and tossing his bowler hat onto the hook behind the door. "I need full concentration for my performance. I did not have it tonight."

Sanjay's tuxedo did look more wrinkled than usual. A couple beads of sweat ran down the side of his face. Come to think of it, I don't think I'd ever seen Sanjay look that disheveled.

"Did anything go wrong?" I asked.

"Not exactly."

"Then what—"

"Never mind. The audience may not have been as wowed by the flaming whisky barrel as they should have been, but I know what my illusions made you realize: the timing of the theft was wrong. When the explosion occurred, the chess set was already gone."

I nodded. "The explosion was a clever way to create the impression that that's when the chess set had been stolen. Just like you were never the shadow on that stage, and you were already gone from the whisky barrel by the time it caught fire. I bet you were gone just as soon as I closed the lid of the barrel."

"I admit nothing," Sanjay said. "But I should have thought of it before this." He shook his head. "It must be the jet lag."

I rolled my eyes as Sanjay picked me up by the elbow.

"Where are we going?"

"You'll see."

Sanjay led me through the maze of the backstage area and out a back door leading to an alley. My eyes had grown accustomed to the backstage light, and I'd forgotten it was only midday. I shielded my eyes from the sun on this cloud-less summer day. We cut through the alley to the front of the theater. Theatergoers streamed out of the main doors, and we cut through them, heading to the box office. But instead of a ticket taker, someone else was waiting for us.

"Astrid," Sanjay said. "I'm glad you could use the com-plementary ticket I left for you."

"How could I resist your message?" she said.

I glared at Sanjay.

"I didn't have time to tell you," he said to me, before turning back to Astrid. "I thought the three of us could take a trip to the police station together."

Astrid's eyes darted angrily between us. Beyond the an-ger, there was fear. She wasn't her normally composed self.

"You conveniently forgot your boyfriend last night," I began. "The one you went to call the morning of the theft."

"Yes, so what?" Astrid said. "Men. They aren't worth remembering." She sneered at Sanjay.

"Some of them are," Sanjay said. "Like the police officers who are going to check your phone records."

Astrid's thin body began to tremble. She looked between us like a cornered animal.

"We know you stole the chess set before the explosion," I said. "When you weren't with Daniella."

"How do you—" Astrid stopped herself.

"As soon as the police learn they have the timing of the theft wrong," I said, "they'll know your alibi doesn't hold up."

"I didn't do it!" Astrid cried. "I only helped."

Sanjay and I glanced at each other. Sanjay's face mirrored the surprise I felt.

"I'm sure the police will be lenient if you tell them who stole the chess set," Sanjay said.

"Don't you see?" Astrid said. "I don't know where the chess set is. I don't even know who I'm working for!"

"But you—"

"I was supposed to leave the key," Astrid said, "and to create a small security problem at the theater, something that Izzy would have to fix—to set him up. Simple! It was supposed to be so simple. Those two little tasks…. I'm turning forty this year, you know. Who wants to hire a forty-year-old model?"

"Come on," Sanjay said, trying to grab Astrid's elbow.

She pulled her arm away. "I won't tell them anything," she said, spitting out the words. "You have no proof, do you? Even though I don't have an alibi, it's not a crime to lie about who I called on the phone."

"Maybe not," I said. "But I wonder if the police would be interested in hearing this?" I pulled my phone out. The "record" button was on.

Astrid's eyes grew wide. She lurched for the phone. Sanjay stepped to my side as I leaped backward away from Astrid's reach. Astrid tripped and fell forward, landing hard on the box office floor. Sanjay took the phone from my hand and slipped it into a hidden pocket of his tuxedo.

At the police station, Astrid was led away for questioning, and I had to leave my phone with the police as evidence. I filled out some paperwork to get it back later. While I was filling out a form, a uniformed constable came up to us.

"Funny case," he said.

"What do you mean?" I asked

"Why would the thief return half of the chess?"

"What?"

"You didn't hear?" he said.

"No," I said, shaking my head and forgetting all about the form in front of me.

"The silver half of the chess set was dropped off by courier earlier this morning."

THIRTEEN

I stretched out my legs over the back of a theater seat, a borrowed laptop from Daniella in my hands. I was hooked up to the wi-fi from the Pizza Hut next door, where I'd eaten several pieces of pizza.

Daniella was off being consoled by Izzy, who had told her he'd watched her show enough times that he knew Astrid's part by heart and could play the part of Alexis as Alex. But even with Izzy filling in, they still didn't have the chess set.

"I can't concentrate with you back there!" Sanjay called out from the stage.

"I thought you wanted me to stay," I called back.

Sanjay hopped down from the stage, walked up the aisle, and sat down next to me. "I can't win," he said. "I can't concentrate either way. You have this mysterious theory that you came up with because the silver half of the chess set was returned. What have you found out?"

"I don't think Clayton Barnes is crazy."

"The philanthropist alchemist guy?" Sanjay said. "Why does his sanity matter? I thought you were going to figure out what happened to the chess set for Daniella's show?"

"That's exactly what I'm doing," I said. "Check it out. Clayton Barnes, the descendant of an old inbred English family who've been wealthy for centuries. A family of selfish jerks who blew all their money gambling and spending lavishly— until Clayton came along. The black sheep of the family with a few screws loose. But he turned their fortune around and was generous at the same time. He's been forgiven by British society and the public because he's from this prominent family and because he's seen as a nice guy in spite of his eccentricities. He's donated millions to various charities, and loaned out many of his gold acquisitions to charities to put on display to raise money from other wealthy donors. In other words, he's done a lot of good."

"That's great history, Jaya. I get it that you're a historian so you like researching this stuff. But what does this have to do with the theft of the chess set?"

"His charities of choice," I said. "They're all arts organizations. They give him memberships and also special invitations to private showings—all to show him his alchemical interest."

"Gold," Sanjay said.

"Exactly. And for every few special gold exhibits he's attended, there's been a theft within the following year."

Sanjay perked up.

"And that's just the exhibits where he's been listed by the press."

"He was casing the places," Sanjay said.

I nodded. "Clayton acted upset about the theft of the gold chess set, but he wasn't nearly as upset until he found out Feisal didn't have insurance. He didn't mean to hurt his friend. That's why he tried to make Izzy look guilty, and why he returned the silver half of the chess set after he learned Feisal hadn't insured it. He wanted Feisal to at least be able to recoup some of his losses. But he kept the gold."

"Sounds like he's even crazier than people think," Sanjay said. "Hoarding all that gold."

"He's not crazy," I said. "He let his guard down with me, since I didn't have any preconceived notions about him. He didn't think I'd look into the theft—in fact, he's been trying awfully hard to convince me to forget about it, and to make Daniella forget about it, too. I don't think he realized how much people cared about Izzy. Izzy isn't turning out to be the simple fall guy he and Astrid thought he would be."

"Hang on," Sanjay said. "How could someone so recognizable pull off all these thefts?"

"Can you tell me what he looks like?" I asked.

"Seriously? He's got to be one of the most recognizable—"

"His *clothes* are recognizable," I said. "And his gold glasses and Sherlock Holmes hat. But what about *him*? Do you know what color eyes he has? Or even what color hair?"

"Do you?" Sanjay said.

"No," I said. "I don't. That's the point. If he takes off those silly 'eccentric' clothes of his, puts on jeans and a dress shirt, and leaves the hat and glasses at home, would anybody recognize him? I doubt it."

"I should have thought of it," Sanjay grumbled.

"This is a calculated plan," I said. "Clayton Barnes is a thief and con artist who's been selling gold treasures to finance his family's crumbling fortune."

FOURTEEN

I shut the computer and looked for my phone to call the police with what I'd found out. After a few seconds of searching through my messenger bag, I remembered the police had my phone.

"Let me use your phone," I said to Sanjay.

"Why?"

"I'm calling the police."

"With your theory that Clayton isn't crazy and is a criminal mastermind?"

"Yes," I said. "But with less dramatic language. Now let me use your phone."

Sanjay punched in some numbers on his phone. I held out my hand, but he refused to hand it to me. A few moments later, he was put through to the detective in charge. I listened as he gave a brief summary of my research—with the key difference being that he said eccentric Clayton Barnes was hoarding gold. When he was done speaking, he listened in silence for almost a minute.

"Oh," he said, frowning. "Yes. Mmm hmm. Yes, of course."

He hung up.

"What is it?"

"It seems," Sanjay said, "that the police have suspected Clayton for quite some time. They put two and two together, just like you did. But they've never been able to prove it. Apparently they're out at his castle right now with a search warrant. Clayton is at the police station and said they were welcome to search his home. That doesn't sound like the reaction of someone who's guilty."

I swore. Why had I thought I could figure out something like this that the police couldn't solve?

"Don't beat yourself up," Sanjay said, putting his hand on my shoulder. "It was a good idea. Too bad both you and the police were wrong."

"I don't think so," I said.

"But didn't you just hear? He's given them permission to search—"

"He's guilty, all right," I said. "But the gold isn't hidden at his mansion where the police can find it."

I stood up.

"Where are you going?" Sanjay asked.

"I'm going to do what I do best. Historical research. I was stupid and arrogant to think I could identify a suspect, when that's what the police do best. But this is what I do best. I know how to find the set and save Daniella's show, clear Izzy from suspicion, and save Feisal's business and his home."

"How?"

"Clayton said he bought his castle because it was once owned by an alchemist. What do you want to bet there are hidden areas of that house the police will never be able to find, even with their thorough search?"

"You've just discovered the police aren't stupid, Jaya. I'm sure they have the blueprints to the house."

"That's where I know more than the police. Historical buildings with something to hide often made fake blueprints. I'm not looking for blueprints, I'm looking for history books about alchemy that mention this historic castle."

Sanjay glanced at his phone. "Five hours until Daniella's show," he said.

"Then we'd better get going."

I knew what I was after, so I was able to find what I was after within hours. The cab we caught at the Edinburgh University library dropped us off around the bend from the castle. We went on foot from there.

Three hours until show time.

The fountain stood where the historical description said it would. Water cascaded down the worn stone, pouring through the waterspout mouths of four gargoyles that faced outward around the circle.

"It's a working fountain," Sanjay said, circling the structure. "I wasn't expecting that. How is that a good entrance to a secret lair?"

"It wouldn't be a very good hiding place if it wasn't working."

"If you tell me I'd have to swim to the bottom of that algae-filled fountain to reach this alchemy lab, I'm going to go get the police. I know that means they'll hang onto the chess pieces as evidence for too long for Daniella and Feisal to use in the show as the draw. But I draw the line somewhere. And that line is slimy algae."

"I'm sure there's a way in that wouldn't leave the alchemists sopping wet when they reach their lab."

"Those historical documents you found didn't say?"

"It wasn't a how-to guide."

Without stepping inside, Sanjay leaned over the edge of the fountain and pressed the nose of the gargoyle in front of him. He leaned back and waited a moment. When nothing happened, he walked around the fountain to the second of two gargoyles and did the same.

If I'd been an alchemist—a real believer—during a time of persecution, I'd have wanted the safest hiding place I could think of for my alchemical lab. Putting it outside the main house, and under a fountain, was a great idea. What else would I do?

I sat down on the stone bench a few feet from the fountain. The bench faced both the fountain and the rose garden that lay beyond it on the way to the mansion. Beauty filled the grounds. Compared to the rest of the ornamentation, the stone bench was rather plain. A stone slab without any flourishes, but it looked like the same centuries-old stone. The flat slab itself was solid, but one of the cobblestones in front of it was loose. I stepped on it and it shifted a little. I knelt down and pressed on it. It moved a little, but didn't give.

"Sanjay," I said. He stood at the last of the gargoyles, scowling at the little monster. "Come over here and put your trap-door skills to use."

"It wouldn't be on the ground," he said. "Too easy for a gardener to accidentally step on. But here..."

He reached his hand under the bench. He ran his fingers along the base for a few moments. When his hand emerged, a faint sound of scraping stone echoed underground. But we didn't see anything.

"Oh, that's ingenious," he said.

"I don't see it."

"It's a two-part mechanism," Sanjay said. "Clayton Barnes hasn't kept up greasing his door very well. We shouldn't have heard that sound. We're supposed to think pushing the button didn't do anything."

"But it didn't."

"Oh yes it did," Sanjay said. "It unlocked the secret passageway."

I stepped aside as Sanjay pushed at the slab of the stone bench. The first side he tried didn't budge. He moved to the other side. The stone swung wide, revealing a narrow set of stone stairs leading down.

FIFTEEN

Sanjay and I looked at each other for a moment before following the steps.

As we descended, it was clear the surrounding shrubbery had been strategically placed around the fountain and bench so that nobody outside of the immediate vicinity would see whoever was taking the hidden staircase.

When my foot hit the bottom step, I felt the stone move. Unlike the loose stone above ground, this stone was sinking. My breath caught and I instinctively backed up, bumping into Sanjay.

Sanjay swore in Punjabi at the same time another noise sounded: The stone bench was closing above us.

That's what the sinking step had done. Sanjay realized it, too. He turned and ran up the steps, but it was too late.

The thick stones came together, closing us off from the world. I don't think of myself as being afraid of the dark, but fear gripped me as pitch black enveloped us. This was definitely not the relaxing vacation I'd signed up for.

The darkness lasted only a few moments. As soon as the stones clicked firmly into place, lights came on. The scene before us was amazing enough that I forgot my fear.

A series of gas lamps hung along the stone walls, but that wasn't what had lighted the room. A set of modern bulbs had been strung along the walls, leading to a room roughly the size of my San Francisco studio apartment.

The room was a combination of old and modern. It hadn't been professionally upgraded. A man of Clayton's wealth could have afforded to do so, but he must have wanted to keep his secret from everyone.

The high-ceilinged room was stocked like an old fashioned chemistry lab. In the back of the cave-like room was a large clay oven. Two stone dragons stood taller than me on either side of the oven. A small trickle of water dripped down one side of the open mouth of the oven. The ceiling in that section of the room was lower than the rest of the room. That wall must have been directly under the fountain. Wooden tables lined the two walls flanking the oven, with crowded shelves above. Glass jars filled with powders of metallic colors, beakers of liquid, metal tongs for lifting hot vessels. In a corner near the oven, a primitive faucet hung over a copper bowl.

"The alchemist's lab," I said. "The fountain even gives it running water."

"It looks like a chemistry lab from Houdini's time," Sanjay said. "He's preserved it perfectly. It's not even dusty."

An acidic smell filled the air. Fresh, not musty. That was curious. Even more curious: a small glass bowl of gold flakes lay on the table closest to us.

One look at Sanjay and I knew he was as confused as me.

"You don't think he actually...?" Sanjay's voice trailed off.

"No," I said, more confidently than I felt. "Definitely not. This isn't real. There has to be a logical explanation."

Sanjay picked up the bowl of gold, raising it to eye level.

"It looks real," he said.

"What do you know about gold?"

"I'm just saying."

"I'm waiting for a host from a reality TV show to jump out from behind the clay oven," I said.

Sanjay walked over to the oven.

"I didn't really mean—" I began.

"I know," he said. "Can I see that magnifying glass you always carry around?"

"You could if it hadn't disappeared with the rest of my luggage." I mentally kicked myself again for putting so many things I didn't want to lose into that checked bag.

"Look at these ashes," Sanjay said, kneeling down. He picked up a handful of blackened ashes and watched them flutter through the air as they slipped through his fingers. "This oven is in use. Why would it be in use if he wasn't practicing alchemy?"

"Burning evidence?" I suggested.

Brushing off his hands, Sanjay considered the idea with a thoughtful expression. "Speaking of which," he said, "I don't see the gold half of a chess set anywhere. You don't think you were wrong about him, do you?"

"No," I said. "My theory makes sense. It's a con. He's hiding something. You saw how well hidden this lab is."

As I spoke the words, I was reminded we were trapped in a room nobody besides Clayton Barnes knew existed. I shivered, and I wasn't sure if it was from the damp chill.

"If he believes he's an alchemist," Sanjay said, "then he believes he needs to hide this lab so he won't be persecuted. I mean really, look at this place—"

"Sanjay," I interrupted. "There's got to be a way out of here, right?"

"Yeah," he said quietly, looking away. "The problem is we need to find it."

"You're good at this stuff," I said. "You found the way in here."

"That was one clever entry system," Sanjay said. "This lab is hidden away below several feet of stone. We need to find the way out ourselves. Nobody is going to find us here."

SIXTEEN

Sanjay's cell phone didn't get any reception, even from the highest step we could climb. For the next thirty minutes, he meticulously tapped every few inches of the walls, floor, and stairway, looking for our way out. I picked up the containers on the tables and went over the table tops and legs. None of it revealed the opening of a secret door. When we regrouped in front of the fireplace, Sanjay's knuckles were raw.

"The stone door we came through is the only way out," he said. "There has to be a trigger, but I'll be damned if I know what it is."

I had been so confident Sanjay would figure it out. I trusted him completely. Just like I knew my own strengths that led us to this alchemy lab, I knew Sanjay's. I hadn't been as frightened as I knew I should have been because I knew he would be able to escape from this room. But what if I was wrong?

Sanjay sighed and sat down on the well-swept floor. He leaned his back against one of the dragons. Watching him, an idea clicked into place in my mind.

"The dragon," I said.

"I already tried it," Sanjay snapped. "I tried everything."

"The black dragon," I said.

"There's no black dragon. They're both gray stone."

"But the scales carved into the stone," I said. "Look at this. There's a black one."

"That's natural discoloration," Sanjay said. "It's been worn…"

His voice trailed off as I pushed on the black scale on the chest of the dragon. It didn't move.

"The black dragon is a meaningful term to alchemists," I said. "Clayton mentioned it, and there was also a tapestry of a black dragon in his castle."

I pushed harder on the black stone. It shifted. The carved stone scale was a lever. The movement dislodged something I hadn't planned on. A large stone fell forward.

I jumped back, but I wasn't fast enough.

The rock smashed into my left arm, a jagged edge tearing through my sweater. I felt the bone break and I screamed.

As searing pain shot through my arm, I realized not only had I broken a bone, but I'd done so while trapped in an underground cave with no cell phone reception, and nobody knew where I was.

"Jaya!" Sanjay cried, pulling me further back from the avalanche. But it was only the one stone that fell.

Pain made its way from my forearm up to my neck. I hadn't broken a bone since I was a kid, but the memories flooded back. I was five years old when I fell out of a tree along the water near our house in Goa. More than the pain, the thing that stuck out in my mind was the difference in what I smelled—I associated a broken arm with fresh air and the scent of bananas, but now the air was stifling and musty. I felt as if I might choke.

"You're bleeding," Sanjay said, kneeling to examine my arm. He pulled a handkerchief out of his pocket. Then another. I must have been seeing double. No, that wasn't it. It was a set of five white handkerchiefs tied together. They must have been for one of his tricks.

"It's broken," I said, my head spinning. I closed my eyes and the sound of scraping stone filled my ears. Was I hallucinating?

"Stay there," he said, as if I was going to go anywhere.

I opened my eyes as a new shot of pain surged through my arm.

Sanjay used the handkerchiefs to tie a wooden spoon from the lab to my arm as a makeshift splint.

"We have to get you out of here," he said. "I'll go over every inch of the room again."

"You don't need to," I said, pointing to the stone stairs with my good arm.

Natural light cascaded over the steps. I hadn't imagined the sound of scraping stone. The doorway down to the lab had opened back up. I'd never been so happy to see the light of day.

"The dragon opened up the door," Sanjay said, following my gaze.

"We didn't hear it because of the falling rock."

"*Come on,*" he said. "I can carry you up the stairs."

"I can walk," I said.

My voice was shaky and I wasn't sure I believed my own words. But the thought of being carried to my rescue like a damsel in distress wasn't much more appealing than being stuck down in that alchemist lab. "I just need a second."

Sanjay held my good arm to help me across the room. Hot pain throbbed each time I took a step. Drops of blood followed in my wake.

"Wait!" I said.

"Do you need me to carry you after all?"

"No," I said, holding my arm in my other hand. I winced in pain. "This is another diversion."

"That's great, Jaya. We can talk about diversions later. Now come on."

"Stop," I said. "I need to think."

"No, you don't," Sanjay said. "You need to get to a hospital."

"Clayton is smart," I said. "Really smart. Just like how he dresses so outrageously so he can hide in plain sight when he wears more normal clothing, this lab is the same false front." I paused and steadied myself on the edge of a table. "If someone happened to find their way into this lab, all it would do is tell them is that he takes his alchemy seriously. Those gold flakes are a prop. This place has another hiding place—the real one."

"That's great, Jaya, but this accident—"

"Don't you get it? That wasn't an accident. It wasn't that a rock was so unstable that it fell when the doorway opened back up. That rock fell because we were too close to his hiding place. It's a booby trap. A booby trap that opens the door back up, for the person who got caught in the trap to be relieved to have a way out—instead of searching for the real hiding place. We were looking for a way out, so we weren't looking for a hiding place. Those dragons are the perfect hiding place."

"You're not going to let this go," Sanjay said.

"No," I said, ignoring the growing bloodstain on the splint wrapped tightly around my arm.

Sanjay's shoulders sagged and he closed his eyes. "All right," he said. "Two minutes. Then we get you out of here."

"The dragon's mouth," I said as I reached the dragon. "The stone tongue is a different piece of stone, not a continuous carving."

Sanjay inspected the mouth of the dragon, grumbling about how I didn't have the magnifying glass I use for historical documents. His grumbling cut off abruptly.

"What is it?" I asked.

"A key hole in the back of the dragon's mouth," he said.

"We don't have the key," I said.

"Who do you think you're talking to?" Sanjay pulled one of the tools from his escape acts and poked it into the dragon's mouth.

A few moments later, a sharp click sounded. Sanjay lifted out the tongue of the dragon. Beyond it were three black velvet bags.

Opening the first drawstring bag, a smile spread across Sanjay's face. He pulled out the gold chess figure of a crazed rook biting his shield.

SEVENTEEN

Two hours later I sat in a reserved box watching *Fool's Gold*.
My arm rested on a pillow in its new cast.

The house was packed. The media was having a field
day with the fact that Clayton Barnes had been arrested for
stealing the gold and silver Lewis Chessmen and was suspected of countless other thefts of gold treasures.

The media attention was great for business. Not only
had Daniella's show sold out all its scheduled performances,
but Feisal had secured a buyer for the chess set.

Sanjay had insisted we go straight to the hospital, rather
than stopping at the theater to hand over the gold chess pieces to Feisal. But while I was getting my cast, Sanjay had called
Feisal who came by to pick up the pieces that Sanjay and I
happened to have "forgotten" were in my bag when we
handed over the other evidence to the police.

"I don't know how to thank you," Feisal had said, bow-
ing and kissing my fingers that poked out from the cast.

Clayton made a full confession after being assured he
would get a deal for returning several missing treasures. He
couldn't return all of the treasures he'd stolen, though. He
hadn't been selling the pieces intact. He's been melting down

treasures in his alchemy lab. It was easier—and safer—to sell gold once it had been disguised.

Clayton's theft of the chess set was never meant to be an impossible crime. His plan had been to have an alibi for the time when the theft was supposed to have taken place, and for Izzy to be the one person without an alibi. With Izzy's past, he was sure the police would have things wrapped up quickly. The German tour group in the hallway ruined the simple plan.

Clayton had used the key, which Astrid left at an appointed spot, to get into the suite and break into the safe early that morning. He'd set an explosion on a timer to go off during the picnic. He was a good thief, and part of his M.O. was that he was exceedingly careful, taking steps such as never having an accomplice know his identity. That's why even though the police had long suspected him, they had never been able to prove anything.

Clayton needed Astrid's key because he hadn't wanted to be seen picking a lock in a crowded hallway. He could open the safe himself, when he had more time and knew Astrid would be making sure the suite's occupants were otherwise occupied. Astrid's other role was to make sure Izzy would be fixing a security problem at the theater while everyone else had the alibi of the picnic. Clayton hadn't counted on Daniella being suspicious of the theater's security breach or of the depth of her feeling for Izzy. That's why he tried to get me to distract Daniella, so we wouldn't look carefully into what had happened.

In retrospect, Clayton should have anticipated human emotions to get in the way, since it was precisely his own feelings that had tripped him up. He knew he would be inconveniencing Feisal by stealing the chess set, but he never imagined Feisal wouldn't have insurance. When he learned Feisal had cut corners and didn't have insurance, he decided to anonymously return the silver half of the chess set, so Feisal could recoup some of his losses. The only reason Clayton had decided on this theft in the first place was because he was desperate. He was running low on funds and didn't see an alternative. He got sloppy.

I heard about Clayton's confession from Feisal when I arrived at the theater from the hospital. Being the good man that he was, Feisal was already talking about forgiving Clayton.

"Is your cast dry yet?" Sanjay asked as the stage lights flickered and signaled that *Fool's Gold* would begin soon.

"I think so," I said. "Why?"

As the lights when down, Sanjay whipped out a black marker from a hidden pocket and signed his name across the cast with a flourish.

Izzy wasn't the greatest actor, but it didn't matter. He wasn't lying when he said he knew the part of Alex, and now that Daniella's usual confidence was back, she had enough talent to carry the show. Besides, half the audience only cared about the sensationalist chess set mystery they were able to be a part of. From the way Daniella and Izzy were looking at each other, Daniella didn't seem to care.

I hadn't ever thought that Sanjay's illusions as The Hindi Houdini could help solve crimes, but it was those clever deceptions of his that had been the key to piecing together how the theft was done. I also hadn't previously thought my research skills as a historian could help catch a criminal, but maybe there was something to it....

I never did get that relaxing vacation I was after. But sitting in the theater box with Sanjay after we'd caught a clever thief, seeing Daniella and Izzy find happiness, and knowing I'd helped save Feisal's antiques business and ensure he'd get to stay in the country that has become home, I wouldn't have had it any other way.

Dear Madison,

You might be wondering why your clothes aren't packed as you left them. I don't normally rifle through the suitcases of others, but this didn't end up being much of a vacation. Instead, your black and white dress (which has been dry cleaned) helped catch a thief who had slipped through the fingers of authorities for years. You can read about it in the Scottish press.

I'm sorry to say I lost the white clutch that went with the dress (I don't know how women keep track of those things!), but I hope the knowledge that your gorgeous clothing was used for good is enough to make up for it. I've also enclosed a small gift for you from Scotland: an Edinburgh Fringe Festival tote bag with a bottle of rare Scotch whisky inside. I wasn't able to go whisky-tasting on this trip as I'd planned (maybe I'll make it back in the future), but I hear it's quite good.

Sláinte – to your health.
Jaya Jones

Diane Vallere

Diane Vallere is a fashion-industry veteran with a taste for murder. *Pillow Stalk*, the first Mad for Mod Mystery was published in October 2012. She also writes the Style & Error Mysteries, juggling both designer fashion and vintage style between the two series. She started her own detective agency at age ten and has maintained a passion for shoes, clues, and clothes ever since. Find her at dianevallere.com.

Be sure to check out Madison's next adventure:
PILLOW STALK
A Mad for Mod Mystery
(available now)

Kendel Lynn

Kendel Lynn is a Southern California native who now parks her flip-flops in Dallas, Texas. She read her first Alfred Hitchcock and the Three Investigators at age seven and has loved mysteries ever since. Her debut novel, *Board Stiff*, won several literary competitions, including the Zola Award for Mystery. Along with writing, she spends her days editing, designing, and figuring out ways to avoid the gym but still eat cupcakes for dinner. Catch up with her at kendellynn.com.

Be sure to check out Elliott's next adventure:
BOARD STIFF
An Elliott Lisbon Mystery
(available April 2013)

Gigi Pandian

Gigi Pandian is the child of cultural anthropologists from New Mexico and the southern tip of India. After being dragged around the world during her childhood, she tried to escape her fate when she left a PhD program for art school. But adventurous academic characters wouldn't stay out of her head. Thus was born the Jaya Jones Treasure Hunt Mystery Series. The first book in the series, *Artifact*, was awarded a Malice Domestic Grant. Find Gigi online at gigipandian.com.

Be sure to check out Jaya's next adventure:
ARTIFACT
A Jaya Jones Treasure Hunt Mystery
(available now)

IF YOU LIKED THIS HENERY PRESS MYSTERY,
YOU MIGHT ALSO LIKE THESE...

Diners, Dives & Dead Ends
by Terri L. Austin

As a struggling waitress and part-time college student, Rose Strickland's life is stalled in the slow lane. But when her close friend, Axton, disappears, Rose suddenly finds herself serving up more than hot coffee and flapjacks. Now she's hashing it out with sexy bad guys and scrambling to find clues in a race to save Axton before his time runs out.

With her anime-loving bestie, her septuagenarian boss, and a pair of IT wise men along for the ride, Rose discovers political corruption, illegal gambling, and shady corporations. She's gone from zero to sixty and quickly learns when you're speeding down the fast lane, it's easy to crash and burn.

Available Now
For more details, visit www.henerypress.com

PORTRAIT of a DEAD GUY

by LARISSA REINHART

In Halo, Georgia, folks know Cherry Tucker as big in mouth, small in stature, and able to sketch a portrait faster than buckshot rips from a ten gauge -- but commissions are scarce. So when the well-heeled Branson family wants to memorialize their murdered son in a coffin portrait, Cherry scrambles to win their patronage from her small town rival.

As the clock ticks toward the deadline, Cherry faces more trouble than just a controversial subject. Between ex-boyfriends, her flaky family, an illegal gambling ring, and outwitting a killer on a spree, Cherry finds herself painted into a corner she'll be lucky to survive.

Available Now
For more details, visit www.henerypress.com

Lowcountry BOIL
by Susan M. Boyer

Private Investigator Liz Talbot is a modern Southern belle: she blesses hearts and takes names. She carries her Sig 9 in her Kate Spade handbag, and her golden retriever, Rhett, rides shotgun in her hybrid Escape. When her grandmother is murdered, Liz high-tails it back to her South Carolina island home to find the killer.

She's fit to be tied when her police-chief brother shuts her out of the investigation, so she opens her own. Then her long-dead best friend pops in and things really get complicated. When more folks start turning up dead in this small seaside town, Liz must use more than just her wits and charm to keep her family safe, chase down clues from the hereafter, and catch a psychopath before he catches her.

Available Now
For more details, visit www.henerypress.com

CROPPED to death

by CHRISTINA FREEBURN

Former US Army JAG specialist, Faith Hunter, returns to her West Virginia home to work in her grandmothers' scrapbooking store determined to lead an unassuming life after her adventure abroad turned disaster. But her quiet life unravels when her friend is charged with murder – and Faith inadvertently supplied the evidence. So Faith decides to cut through the scrap and piece together what really happened.

With a sexy prosecutor, a determined homicide detective, a handful of sticky suspects and a crop contest gone bad, Faith quickly realizes if she's not careful, she'll be the next one cropped.

Available Now
For more details, visit www.henerypress.com

FRONT PAGE FATALITY

by LynDee Walker

Crime reporter Nichelle Clarke's days can flip from macabre to comical with a beep of her police scanner. Then an ordinary accident story turns extraordinary when evidence goes missing, a prosecutor vanishes, and a sexy Mafia boss shows up with the headline tip of a lifetime.

As Nichelle gets closer to the truth, her story gets more dangerous. Armed with a notebook, a hunch, and her favorite stilettos, Nichelle races to splash these shady dealings across the front page before this deadline becomes her last.

Available January 2013
For more details, visit www.henerypress.com

I9781938383106
MYSTERY OTH
Other people's baggage :

PROSPECT FREE LIBRARY
915 Trenton Falls St.
Prospect, New York 13435
(315)896-2736

MEMBER
MID-YORK LIBRARY SYSTEM
Utica, N.Y. 13502

150100

PRA 02/1/13 Mav. advance